Bello:

hidden talent rediscovered

Bello is a digital only imprint of Pan Macmillan,
established to breathe new life into previously published,
classic books.

At Bello we believe in the timeless power of the imagination,
of good story, narrative and entertainment and we want to use
digital technology to ensure that many more readers
can enjoy these books into the future.

We publish in ebook and Print on Demand formats
to bring these wonderful books to new audiences.

www.panmacmillan.co.uk/bello

Eileen Dewhurst

An only child, Eileen Dewhurst was self-sufficient and bookish from an early age, preferring solitude or one-to-one contacts to groups, and hating sport. Her first attempts at writing were not auspicious. At 14, a would-be family saga was aborted by an uncle discovering it and quoting from it choked with laughter. A second setback came a few years later at school, when a purple passage was returned with the words 'Cut this cackle!' written across it in red ink: a chastening lesson in how embellishments can weaken rather than strengthen one's message.

Eileen read English at Oxford, and afterwards spent some unmemorable years in 'Admin' before breaking free and dividing her life in two: winters in London doing temporary jobs to earn money and experience, summers at home as a freelance journalist, spinning 'think pieces' for the *Liverpool Daily Post* and any other publications that would take them, and reporting on food and fashion for the long defunct *Illustrated Liverpool News*, as well as writing a few plays.

Her first sustained piece of writing was a fantasy for children which was never published but secured an agent. Her Great Autobiographical Novel was never published either, although damned with faint praise and leading to an attempt at crime writing that worked: over the next thirty years she produced almost a book a year and also published some short stories in anthologies and *Ellery Queen's Mystery Magazine*.

Eileen has always written from an ironic stance, never allowing her favourite characters to take themselves too seriously: a banana skin is ever lurking.

Eileen Dewhurst

ROUNDABOUT

First published in 1998 by Severn House

This edition published 2014 by Bello
an imprint of Pan Macmillan, a division of Macmillan Publishers Limited
Pan Macmillan, 20 New Wharf Road, London N1 9RR
Basingstoke and Oxford
Associated companies throughout the world

www.panmacmillan.co.uk/bello

ISBN 978-1-4472-5695-3 EPUB
ISBN 978-1-4472-5694-6 POD

Visit **www.panmacmillan.com** to read more about all our books
and to buy them. You will also find features, author interviews and
news of any author events, and you can sign up for e-newsletters
so that you're always first to hear about our new releases.

Chapter One

The hooker reflected in the cheval glass was on the way over the hill, but had the looks still to stop a needy man in his tracks. And with the soft coaxing voice which was murmuring to her image, would be likely to keep him beside her even when he had taken it in that she was not quite so young as she had appeared at a distance. Face and figure were ripely attractive—Phyllida passed her hands down her unassisted body in a rare gesture of self-satisfaction—and there was promise of a not unrefined experience in the eyes and parted lips.

Shivering now, with the invariable mingling of fear and satisfaction which always told her that her transformation was as total as she could make it, Phyllida shimmied across to her bedroom window and stood looking out.

She saw first, as she always did, the huge spread of sky spanning the open sea that she loved and from which after long exile she was separated at last by no more than a short slope and a promenade. Now the sky was featureless grey, broken by a lemon-coloured slit low down on the darker grey horizon which was sending thin fingers of light towards her across the leaden surface of the water. A lamb-like Sunday afternoon in March after days of leonine wind that had flung her from lamp-post to lamp-post. One got used to most things in life, good and bad, but she would never get used to the exhilaration, the absolute marvel, of living so close to the sea . . .

For an absurd, unworldly second the car parked at her gate seemed puny and unimportant, and then Phyllida saw that its driver was on the narrow path to her door, was stumbling on the edge of it as his gaze swept her windows, and was the producer of the TV drama series for which she was soon to start filming in London.

Deploring her brief lapse from professionalism Phyllida darted backwards, then stood motionless, awaiting the inevitable doorbell and deciding in the seconds before it came that she wouldn't answer it. Would give a chance, at least, to the possibility that she had backed off in time.

But after the second ring she heard the rattle of the locked side gate, and when she moved a cautious few steps back towards the window she saw that Patrick Varley was standing just inside the front gate with a mobile phone to his ear and looking grimly up at her bedroom window.

He was showing her that he was about to ring the police, and Phyllida threw herself downstairs and across the hall.

'You'd better come in, Patrick,' she called out as she opened the front door, 'and I'll try to explain.'

Half a dozen long strides had him beside her. Gripping her arm.

'Look,' he said, easing his grasp as she offered no resistance. 'This house belongs to Miss Phyllida Moon, and if you're here with her consent'—the scepticism in his eyes hardened into disbelief as they raked her—'then why didn't you answer the doorbell?'

'Because I hoped you hadn't seen me. Patrick—'

He stiffened, registering this time that she had used his name. 'You know her. So where is she?'

'Standing in front of you. Patrick, I'm Phyllida. For goodness sake shut the door and I'll explain.'

'You can explain with the door open.' The disbelief was still there, sharing place now with impatience.

Phyllida shook her right arm free and pulled off the wig as she leaned past him to slam the door shut with her left.

'Listen to my voice! I'm Phyllida Moon, Patrick, actress engaged by Harrison Productions Ltd to play the part of a private eye in their imminent series *A Policeman's Lot*. Which is the reason you're here, no doubt.'

'Yes,' But he had backed away from her, was looking at her with a shocked surprise which, as she registered it, matched her own.

2

'And I find you . . . I'm not surprised you didn't want me to discover your second career.'

'I do have a second career,' Phyllida agreed. She had wondered how she would feel if a moment came when she had to give away her secret, and in these ridiculous and embarrassing circumstances she was discovering that she felt nothing beyond an intense eagerness for it to be accepted. 'I'm a private eye in real life, Patrick. With a difference from the series, I sleuth in character. I've been given an assignment to find the whereabouts of a local tart who's gone missing and I'd just completed my rehearsal of my transformation when you arrived.' She hadn't got through. 'Look. Find Peter Piper Private Investigator in Yellow Pages or the telephone book. He's my boss and he tends to spend Sunday afternoons in his cosy office in Dawlish Square. His home number's ex-directory, so if he isn't in the office it won't do me much good to give it to you. But try the office. Or lock me in the bathroom for a few moments with some of my own clothes.'

'Phyllida . . .' She had made it. 'Neither of those things will be necessary.'

'If you're sure . . .?' She was half joking. It had been a nasty few moments, but they were over. 'I took the job to get hands-on experience for the series, and stayed on because I liked it. Look, make yourself at home in there'—Phyllida indicated the sitting-room—'and I'll go up to the bathroom anyway, I don't feel good like this.'

He grinned, 'I can believe you. Sorry.'

'It was a lot to swallow,' she called down from the landing. 'That's why I didn't answer the door.'

'A pity you're not sleuthing in character for the series,' Patrick said, blinking and grinning, as she joined him ten minutes later.

Because you're so very ordinary when you're you, Phyllida mentally completed for him. 'I'm happy with the series as it is,' she said aloud. 'Though it would be easier working in character there than among real people. Deceiving them. Perhaps hurting them.' *Hurting myself.* She thought, as she tried not to, of the potentially nice men from whose lives she had suddenly disappeared.

'Um, how does it work? I mean, if you're asked for your address and or telephone number?'

'All my characters stay at the Golden Lion, Seaminster's nicest hotel if not its smartest. Opposite my office in Dawlish Square. That's where my subjects pick my characters up and put them down. I've a permanent room there which I can use to transform in, and which I have to use if someone tells me they're going to telephone very late or very early.'

'You never give this address?'

She knew her alarm had spread to her face. 'Good God, no. My home and myself are my anonymity. If there's any chance I've aroused suspicions and may be followed I'll leave my character in the hotel.' She leaned towards him. 'You're the only person in the world, Patrick, beyond my boss, my colleagues and the staff at the hotel who knows my secret.'

'I'll keep it.'

'You must. Please.' Oh, she hadn't realised until this moment how vulnerable she was. 'No exceptions. Not even your nearest and dearest. Promise?'

'Of course. But I don't promise not to ask you more questions, or suggest we might bring the situation into a play or another series. It has to be unique.'

'But we wouldn't know, would we?' Studying his plump sensible face, she thought she should be able to trust him. 'What did you want to talk about?'

'Nothing urgent. I was along the coast for lunch, and came on spec.' All at once he was the uncomfortable one. 'And I'm just realising I should probably apologise for arriving unannounced on a Sunday afternoon.'

'That's all right, I'm glad to see you, even if I'm uneasy at having been rumbled. It's the first time.'

'I've told you, Phyllida, I'll keep shtoom. Now, our timetable's getting more precise, to the extent where you can commit yourself to a short let, and I think I've found a flat which would suit you. I was going to suggest you took it a few weeks before we start, while you looked around for somewhere to buy in or near London, but now ...' Patrick glanced round the small bright room with what Phyllida saw as reluctant approval. 'You talked about a second career? You're going to keep it on?'

'Yes. When I'm not wanted at the studio. And I've no guarantee I'll be wanted for a second series. Or any other TV work. That's not a question!' Phyllida went on quickly, feeling the flush of her modesty in her cheeks as Patrick looked down at his shoes. 'I'm only telling you that if I can keep my second career going to my boss's satisfaction it's guaranteed for as long as I want it. But it'll still come second to whatever Harrison Productions may want of me. Fair enough?'

'Couldn't be fairer. This house—is it yours?'

'Yes!' Phyllida couldn't quite keep her satisfaction out of her voice. After an adult life spent in digs or rented accommodation with the husband she had lately walked out on, she still hadn't got used to the miracle of owning her own home.

'Nice,' Patrick commented, unpatronisingly. And he was a nice man, Phyllida reflected. Old-fashioned in appearance and manners (those shoes he had lowered his eyes to were polished black leather), perhaps modelling himself, consciously or unconsciously, on one of the actor-managers of the past (the dark coat he had at last taken off had an astrakhan collar), but shrewd, as she had already discovered, in his approach to modern drama. 'But I can't resist asking, why Seaminster?'

'My last straight acting job was with a company who ended their summer season here last year. My husband was the stage manager and—we decided to split up.' As they should have done a lot sooner, only she hadn't been able to walk away until she had actually seen him with one of his other women. 'I was born and spent my childhood on the Cornish coast and, well, I just like being here. I'm trying to write a history of women and the stage, and London didn't seem to offer any particular advantage over Seaminster for that. Or for getting a job with a private eye. I'd got my contract with Harrison Productions before I decided to stay on when the company left, buy the house I was renting. But I'll like coming to London, Patrick.'

'You must have a very accommodating boss.'

'I have. And one who was getting along nicely before I appeared, he didn't need another member of staff. I offered a luxury service he can manage without.'

'And one it's unlikely anyone else could offer. So you'll have peace of mind during your leaves of absence. That will be essential, Phyllida, if you're to give your best.'

Patrick's authority was all the more effective for being so rarely and so gently exercised. 'I know that,' Phyllida responded quickly. 'I'll give it.' She got to her feet. 'And now let me give you tea or something stronger before you start back to London.'

'Thanks. Tea, please. You'll have all the temptations in the way of more conventional actors and actresses,' Patrick said musingly, as a few minutes later Phyllida put a mug into his hand. 'How d'you cope if you get emotionally involved with someone the job's decreeing you make up to?'

'I don't. I mean, I don't get involved. I can't, Patrick. And if you think, it's easier for me than for actors on stage. They don't fall for characters, they fall for each other. The people I meet can only fall for the character I'm playing so even if I . . . like someone, it won't be Phyllida Moon they like in return.'

'That could be sad.'

'It could be,' Phyllida responded, with determined lightness of tone. It already had been, a couple of times, when she had had to destroy a character which had endeared itself to a subject who might, in ordinary circumstances, have endeared himself to her. So it had helped, in a depressing kind of way, to know in each case that it was not Phyllida Moon who was the object of desire.

'It would be difficult anyway, technically, with wigs and make-up and so on,' Phyllida said. 'So even in character I have to keep things at arms' length.'

'You won't be able to do that in *A Policeman's Lot*, with your paramour tearing in and out, but TV make-up for modern productions is minimal nowadays . . . Could you come up to London fairly soon, meet him and other members of the cast and production team? We'll book you into a hotel, and show you the flat. It's in Tooting, a good spot for anyone coming up from the coast.'

Phyllida pondered. 'I'm' going to Clapham next week for my first encounter as the character who opened the door to you. I haven't anything needing me round the clock at the moment and I think I could stay over for a night or two. I promise to change before presenting myself at the studio.'

Chapter Two

Carol intercepted the casserole dish before her daughter could get her hands on it. That's all right, darling. You go and talk to Daddy, sit down and have a drink with him. I can manage.'

'Don't treat me like a visitor!' Sally said sharply. 'Please, Mum!'

'I'm sorry.' Carol Hargreaves yearned with affection as she watched Sally's pale face flame red and her lower lip start to tremble, the outward expression of an inward disarray she had first seen when Sally was toddling. 'I didn't mean to.'

'Which makes it *worse!*' Sally flung out of the kitchen and into the sitting-room, where she cast herself down on the sofa and deliberately sprawled.

Carol put the casserole back into the oven and followed her. 'But that's what you are now, isn't it, Sal?'

'No! And not you too, Dad!'

For the first time Sally could remember, her father had got to his feet as she entered the sitting-room and was smiling politely at her as if she was a guest.

'You don't live here any more,' Carol pointed out.

'I'll always live here.' It was almost a wail, and over her drooping head Carol and Matthew exchanged glances. 'Are you trying to punish me for going to live with Jeremy?'

'Of course not, darling!' A second exchange of looks between the parents. Was that, perhaps, what they had been doing? 'But it's bound to change things a bit.'

'Going to take my front door key off me, are you?'

'Oh, Sally, don't be an idiot!' Carol sat down beside her daughter and put an arm round her shoulders. 'Of course not. Ever, ever,

ever. But . . . Daddy and I have to get used to the new situation, you have to realise that.' Carol paused, anxious to get it right. And you have to realise . . . we're starting to see you now as a person in your own right. A person due—courtesies.'

'For goodness sake, Mum!'

But to Carol's relief Sally was laughing, tumbling into her arms and hugging her. Then getting up to hug her father. That's great of you both. Let's hope I deserve it. But I'll always want to have my cake and eat it so far as this house is concerned. However greedy that may be.'

'We'd hate it any other way.' Matthew had sat down again. 'We've just got to adjust, you see, Sal. We as well as you. Which brings me to ask you if your adjustment's going as you'd hoped. Is it?'

'Oh, yes, Dad!'

Neither anxious parent could see any extra cause for anxiety in their daughter's instant emphatic response, her sudden radiant and reminiscent smile. It was, in fact, a perfect response in the circumstances, the only one they had hoped for, and so in each of them it evoked a brief pang of jealousy and sorrow which both managed to keep out of their own smiles. 'We're so glad for you,' they chorused, and Sally laughed again.

'There you go, coming out with exactly the same thing at the same time. You've done that as long as I can remember.'

'Would you like to be doing that with Jeremy when your daughter leaves home?' Carol asked, mentally rounding on herself the moment she had spoken for not being content with what Sally had given them.

Sally wriggled irritably beside her. 'Oh, Mum! No happy ever afters, please! I don't know. How can I know? People never have known, but they have the sense today to admit it and not go rushing into long-term commitments. Perhaps when marriage vows start to reflect reality—ask you to say you'll *try* to stick together rather than that you *will*—perhaps then younger people'll be more inclined to think about signing that piece of paper.'

The parents' eyes met, and Carol saw Matthew's shoulders rise and fall, 'Fair enough, Sally,' he said, getting up and ambling over to the corner cupboard. 'Now, let's drink to you and Jeremy being happy now.'

During the meal they talked about other things.

'How's the library?' Carol asked, as she matched the last piece of biscuit on her plate to the last crumb of cheese. Her current most endearing image of her daughter was of seeing her one afternoon at the enquiry desk in Seaminster's small public library: a slim, neat girl with a lot of dark hair falling over her face as she leaned towards a computer screen then looked up with a smile at the person who had asked for her help.

'The library's fine. And it's good being able to get there on foot.' From the inland parental home, Sally had had a half-hour car journey.

'You can walk by the sea part of the way, can't you?' Carol hadn't actually seen her daughter on the early morning promenade, but her mental picture was vivid.

'Yes. That's great. I'll show you ... When exactly are you and Maggie starting your holiday?'

'The day after tomorrow. Monday. Sometime in the afternoon.'

'Jeremy and I want you both to have dinner with us at least once while you're in Seaminster. Will you be able to manage Tuesday night? I'm told the food's quite good at the Fountains but I've just booked you bed and breakfast so you won't be tied.'

'Except for Thursday—our art class—we'll be able to manage any night that suits you and Jeremy. The point about this holiday, darling, is to be uncommitted. I'm going to find fresh inspiration for my book jackets and Maggie's taking a rest from Ross—they've managed to book him into the home near Brighton where he was all right the last couple of times she and Frank went away.'

'Great.' Sally had looked discreetly at her watch a couple of times since Carol had brought the cheese in, and now looked at it openly. 'Ten o'clock! Jeremy will think I've abandoned him.'

'I'll get the coffee right away. It was nice of you to come on your own,' Carol said, then added hastily that that didn't mean she and Daddy didn't like Jeremy, didn't want him to come to dinner too.

'I know, Mum, I know.' Sally leaned across the table. 'Look, we're being a bit careful all of a sudden what we say to one other and how we say it. We mustn't get into the habit. You and Dad and me! It would be awful.'

'Oh, darling!' Carol took the outstretched hand, remembering the recent flushed face and trembling lip and marvelling that her daughter could be so childish one minute and so sensible and adult the next. 'It would.'

'Thank you, Sally,' Matthew said. This time he and Carol looked at one another with pleasure.

But when Sally had whirled off, the light of anticipation in her eyes, they came back to the supper table in a deflated silence, finishing off the coffee and looking a bit bleakly round the remains of the feast.

'I think it's rather nice,' Matthew said at last, after studying his wife's face for a few moments in silence, 'that when you told Sally you and Maggie were taking a break she was so insistent you took it in Seaminster.'

Carol's sombre face lit up. 'I know. And I'm all the more determined while I'm there not to give the impression of wanting to interfere in her new life. I was going to invite them both to dinner at the hotel or somewhere else they like—still will—but I'm awfully happy Sally got in first.'

'I know.' Matthew leaned across the table to pat her hand, then got to his feet. 'Come on! Let's get tidied up and off to bed.'

They shared the washing up and putting away, as they always did. And as he always did, Matthew announced as his last act of the day that he'd just pop into the garage for a moment to make sure he'd remembered to put all his tools away. Matthew was an architect, and Carol sometimes wished he drew as a hobby too so that they could talk as a couple of practitioners. But although his main nonprofessional occupation was creative he worked only with wood. One summer night, having followed him out of the house to perform some last chore in the garden, on an impulse of curiosity

Carol had peered through the window at the back of the garage where he had his work bench, and watched him add a few tender strokes of the plane to a piece of the fallen laburnum which had taken so long to be nursed to the right state for turning into one of his sculptures. Now, each evening, she pictured him, creatively satisfied by a brief conjunction of tool and object.

Tonight, though, there was something of her own she needed to do, and in private, and she hoped he might take a little longer than usual, or linger downstairs. The moment he had left the house on his usual pretext she plunged upstairs, flopped down on the bed, picked up the telephone and punched out a number.

Carol saw her face in the long glass opposite as she listened to the ringing tone and was shocked at its tension, its furtive look. Not a face for Matthew to see, she told herself, trying to relax it.

When the call was eventually answered it relaxed of its own accord. 'It's you. Good. I just wanted to tell you . . .' Carol stopped to listen. 'No, I don't need to, do I? Oh, if only . . . I've started to feel scared, somehow, and I can't—'

She was unlucky. Matthew was in the doorway, a smiling enquiry in his face.

'All right, Maggie,' Carol said cheerily to the handset. 'That seems to be everything sorted. I'll pick you up on Monday at about eleven. Love to Frank.' Matthew mouthed a few words. 'Love from Matthew, he's just come into the room. Bye, now.'

Phyllida liked the feel of the street, with its small but solid Victorian terraces and regularly spaced pavement trees just breaking into bud. But it wasn't a street into which her character, Marilyn, fitted, and when the taxi decanted her at Number Fourteen she ran quickly across to the low iron gate and up the short path beyond.

To Phyllida's relief, her ring at the bell was answered immediately.

But the respectable-looking young woman at the door was staring at her in horror and narrowing the gap she had initially opened between door and post.

'Binkie Page?' Marilyn inquired, thrusting herself into what was left of the space. She was the sort of woman in whom a lack of welcome engenders aggression rather than diffidence.

'My name is Mrs Brenda Barker,' the woman responded, with a mixture of pride and primness which Phyllida, somewhere in the excluded recesses of her own mind, found amusing.

'Née Miss Binkie Page?' Marilyn suggested. 'For goodness' sake let me in, dear, you obviously don't like me on the step.'

Mrs Barker hesitated, glancing beyond Phyllida to the taxi.

'It's all right,' Marilyn assured her. 'I'm not planning on staying. Just want a word.' Mrs Barker made no move. 'Look, if you don't have it with me, dear, someone else will come.'

'I don't know you,' Mrs Barker said stiffly.

'Don't you? Well, best sometimes to have a short memory.'

'I mean it, I don't know you! Even when I . . .'

'When you was on the streets alongside of me? Well, could be you don't, I ain't been in town long. Maybe that's why I drew the short straw. Got told to look for you. The girls is worried about you, Binkie. That's all it is, I ain't gonna bite you. Better let me in, dear.'

Mrs Barker looked worriedly up and down the empty road. 'All right.' The gap between door and door post slowly widened. 'Just for a minute.'

The interior of the house looked as instantly respectable as the householder. Mrs Barker led Phyllida through a narrow hall into a sitting-room comfortably if inexpensively furnished with a three-piece suite too large for it and a few reproductions of well-known pictures on the flower-sprigged walls. She motioned to one of the armchairs and sat down stiffly on the edge of the other.

'I don't understand,' she said, smoothing her knee-length skirt, 'how you found me.'

This was the tricky bit. 'I didn't, I'm just the messenger boy. Pat—you know Pat?' Grudgingly Mrs Barker nodded. 'Pat told me she'd had a bit of luck, met someone apparently who told her to try this address. Don't ask me who it was because I don't know. And don't for heaven's sake worry about it, if you're OK that's

OK by Pat and the girls. They—we—just wanted to make sure you wasn't lying in some dark alley. Honest.' Her character's smile could be persuasive when she liked, and Phyllida judged this the moment to bring it out.

Mrs Barker bridled slightly in its rays and settled herself a little more comfortably in her chair. 'Yes . . . well . . . That's nice, if it's really what you say.'

'God's honour,' Marilyn assured her. 'And you'd've done the same the other way on if you'd had the chance.'

'Yes . . .'

No, you wouldn't, Phyllida interpreted. *You haven't got Pat's generosity of soul.* 'There you are, you see.' Marilyn smiled again. 'Like to tell me what it's all about? Pat and the girls'd appreciate it.'

'All right.' A look of self-satisfaction was creeping into Mrs Barker's face. 'Just for a minute.'

'The length of a cuppa?' Marilyn suggested.

This time, to Phyllida's pleased surprise, her smile was returned. 'Why not? But your taxi . . .'

'That's all right, I told him I could be a few minutes.'

'You might as well come through, then.'

Phyllida followed Mrs Barker to the back of the house, and into a small, very clean and tidy kitchen.

'I gather you won't be coming back, then?' she said, as her hostess picked up the kettle.

Mrs Barker shuddered. 'No. I won't ever be coming back. I been lucky,' she admitted in a rush. 'I met a guy when I wasn't . . . when I wasn't working, and he never realised. I told him I was unemployed, had been a cleaner. That was true once, anyway.' She looked defiantly at Phyllida, as if she might be about to deny it. 'He's a nice boy. I can't say as how I . . . well, I can't see myself ever feeling romantic, like, after everything, but I know a good thing and he's awful kind and generous. He married me.'

Mrs Barker looked at Phyllida with wide, astonished eyes, obviously not yet over the surprise of her good luck. Phyllida gave an appropriate long-drawn-out whistle.

'Yes,' Mrs Barker said, turning away to make the tea. 'He married me. Just three weeks after we'd met. I'd stopped work within a few days, feeling I knew the way the wind was blowing. But anyway, even if I'd been wrong . . . I just sort of couldn't, any more. Couldn't have anything to do with any of it, or any of you, if you'll forgive me speaking plainly. That's why I never told Pat, just disappeared. I was wrong, I knew I was wrong at the time, but, well . . .' Mrs Barker turned back to Marilyn, the return of suspicion tightening the face which Phyllida was beginning to think was quite pretty. 'You sure you just come to see I'm all right?'

'God's honour Binkie. Sorry, what did you say your name was?'

'Brenda! It's on my birth certificate!'

'I'm sure. Well, Brenda,' Phyllida picked up the mug of tea Mrs Barker had pushed towards her along the work top. 'Here's to you. From me and Pat and the girls. We all wish you well. Wish there was the same happy ending for the rest of us.'

'Perhaps, there will be.' The smile again.

'Here's to that, too.' Phyllida took another reluctant sip of the strong brew. 'Pat asked me to tell you she's always there if you want her, but she won't come looking for you. None of us will again, seeing how things are.'

'I'm sorry,' Brenda said. 'You're all great. It's just . . .'

'Just that you've moved on. Good Lord, girl, we understand that! Just wanted to be sure it was what you wanted, that you wasn't being forced into anything. Including respectability.'

Marilyn laughed at her own joke, and Brenda just managed to join in.

'Your hubby still don't know about—anything?' Marilyn asked, as Brenda led the way to the front door.

'No! And I don't feel . . . I feel safer now, sort of, since you've come. I've not felt quite right, quite fair. And now you all know the score . . .'

'We'll respect it. Of course. Now,' Marilyn said, turning as they reached the door and holding out her hand. Brenda took it without hesitation. I'll put my head down and make a dirty dive. You shut the door right away.'

'Thanks. You're good.' To Phyllida's astonishment she was suddenly enveloped in a brief bear hug.

'Hey, hey! Mind the war-paint!' It was another pleasant surprise that Brenda had forgotten to be wary of it. 'You're all right, I think,' Marilyn said, studying her. 'Some powder on your collar. Go and have a look, make sure.'

'Thanks.' For the second time Brenda Barker was hesitating at her front door.

'For heaven's sake let me out, girl! Good luck!'

Phyllida flung herself down the path, across the pavement, and into the back of the taxi.

'Where to now?' It was a relief that the taxi driver, an elderly man, was looking at her in his mirror with exasperation rather than interest.

'Victoria, please.'

It seemed the nearest place able to provide both the facilities and the anonymity that she needed. When she had restored herself, and telephoned Peter, she would get another taxi to the studios.

Maggie Trenchard felt no better downstairs than she had felt lying in bed after waking. It wasn't her heart, this time, although that had been playing up lately and she was starting to face a possibility that she would never make old bones. No, the feeling she had now was in her mind, a sense of dread all the more ridiculous because she was free of Ross for a week and about to go on holiday with Carol. Not that she wanted to be free of Ross, Maggie told herself as she moved draggingly around the kitchen—perhaps that was the trouble with her that morning, she had time for once to think about herself—but the constant care she had to give him was very draining and there was no doubt he was getting worse. Both the doctor and Frank had begun to urge her to agree to his going permanently into Dorsey House, but despite feeling so tired always she wasn't ready for such a drastic and—she couldn't help feeling—unnatural step. Ross was her only child, who had not asked to be born in any shape or form, let alone the grotesque travesty of mind and body with which she and Frank had endowed him. So Ross must remain her care and concern, although she was looking forward to a week without him. A week at the seaside with her best friend and without Frank . . .

Maggie jerked guiltily as Frank came in, immediately dominating the kitchen as his expansive presence tended to dominate any room he entered. Not that Frank was an especially big man, Maggie vaguely thought as she automatically smiled a welcome, although he was fit and strong. It was just, perhaps, that he couldn't imagine being unwelcome anywhere . . . and seldom was, she supposed, with his optimistic outlook and ready banter. She wished, though, that he wouldn't have his hair cut quite so short, his strong face had no need of such macho emphasis. Once, she remembered, with an inward start of surprise (it seemed such a very long time ago), when he had let it grow and it had been soft and silky, she had liked to run her fingers through it . . .'

'Morning, love,' Frank said. Then lookedrat her more closely than usual, evoking in her another start of guilt. 'You look a bit pale. But interesting.' He crossed the kitchen and put his hand on her bottom, gently pinching it. 'You all right?'

Carol would probably be able to tell Matthew that she was battling against a stupid sense of dread. She couldn't tell Frank anything like that. 'Just a bit of a headache, it'll lift when I've had a couple of tablets with my coffee. Toast coming up.'

Frank spent the few moments he sat with her at the kitchen table grumbling about the current staff at his garage.

'Apart from brother Daniel there's not a man jack among them doing the jobs the way I'm prepared to do them. *Do* do them, half the time. Think I'm going to have to have a clean sweep before long if things don't improve. Well, better get myself over there for another pep talk. What time are you off?'

'I'm picking Carol up about eleven.' Maggie was still in love with her new car and enjoyed driving. Carol did, too, but was considerate enough to let Maggie do the things she remained strong enough to cope with.

'I'll miss you, Maggie.'

'It's only for a week.'

'Yeah.' He was on his feet, standing behind her chair with his big hands on her shoulders. According to you and Carol, your two beaux at the art class will miss you too.'

They both laughed. 'They're easy enough to keep in their place,' Maggie assured him. 'Just a couple of likely lads.'

'Oh, I don't mind my wife being fancied by other men,' Frank assured her in his turn. 'Gives me a bit of a buzz, as a matter of fact. So long as you save all your kisses for me, as the song goes. Take it easy while you're away, Maggie. Don't overdo things. Promise?'

'I promise, Frank.'

'Good girl.' He pulled her chair back and obediently Maggie got to her feet, turned to face him and entered his embrace. It was affectionate for once rather than sexy and she didn't find it difficult because she was fond of Frank, he was a good husband and he made her laugh.

In fact she hugged him to her. '*You* take care of *yourself*. There should be all the food you need in the freezer. Just—'

He ran his fingers through the red-gold hair, kissed the tip of the freckled nose. 'I know, I know. And I'll have what I want. I expect I'll eat at the club some nights.'

'Good. You'll enjoy the company.' Maggie hesitated. 'Frank . . . will you . . .?'

He studied her anxious face with a knowing half smile. 'I'll go and see Ross. Of course.'

'Thank you, darling.' Maggie put her relief and gratitude into her final kiss, and as he left the house Frank's smile was broad.

Chapter Three

'Only a let, Peter,' Phyllida assured her boss, affectionately amused, as so often, by the expressiveness of his thin, boyish face, at present registering wide-eyed anxiety. And only for the actual times I'm working. I've no intention of living anywhere but Seaminster. Or taking any permanent job apart from this one.'

The anxiety disappeared in a grin. 'That's a relief, thanks for telling me. It was just that I couldn't help wondering, once you got there and met everyone . . . The glamour . . .' Peter ended vaguely. Then quickly resumed. 'Not that you're the sort of person to be influenced by glamour, but you'll be at the centre of it, and I just thought—'

'I'm extremely privileged in two directions,' Phyllida interrupted. 'And you're very generous and understanding to be prepared to let fne go when I'm summoned by the other. I'd feel guilty if I didn't know I was a luxury as far as Peter Piper Private Investigator is concerned.'

'I'd have agreed with you once.' Peter said judicially. 'But it's like an increase in one's income, it starts off as a luxury and then becomes one's way of life. We'll be very aware of your absence when you're not here, Phyllida. But we'll be very proud of you too. Very star-struck.'

'Jenny and Steve a bit, perhaps.' Phyllida conceded reluctantly, meeting Peter's reminiscent smile with an involuntary smile of her own. Young Steve had already proved his suggestibility by developing a crush on the maturely attractive American lady with the Lauren Bacall look whom Phyllida had several times brought into being. 'But I don't want anything like that from any of you.' She meant it. 'I just want my place kept warm.' Phyllida realised on a stab of alarm that if Peter found another woman to sleuth in character she would be painfully jealous, an emotion she was not at home with. Which was perhaps why it had taken her so long to walk out on Gerald . . .

'And so it will be. But you've a few weeks yet?' The anxiety was creeping back.

'Six. Everything's behind schedule, as I gather it so often is with TV enterprises. So, six at least.'

'Great.' Peter's radiant smile flashed on and off as he pushed back the flop of brown hair which immediately resumed its fall over his forehead. 'Now . . .' He slid the usual slim folder across his desk. 'You've wound up the case of the missing tart, for which much thanks. This, I think, is a rather more intriguing one. Perhaps because it sounds so unlikely.'

'Tell me about it.' Phyllida felt the familiar surge of adrenaline as she laid her hand on the folder. She wouldn't open it until Peter had told her what it contained, and she was on her own.

'Right. Steve as well, on this one, so I told him to be here at eleven.' Which it precisely was, Phyllida saw on Peter's wall clock. But he always managed to time his seemingly spontaneous chat to culminate relevantly at an exact moment.

A second or two after Peter had pressed his buzzer Steve appeared, holding the door for Jenny who bore a tray containing three mugs of coffee. 'As you said to come in,' Steve explained, pointing to a mug, with a self-deprecation Phyllida found suspect.

'All right, Steve. And thanks, Jenny. We'll fill you in,' he added encouragingly as, with a wistful smile over her shoulder, Jenny went back to the door and closed it behind her. 'Sit down, Steve. Two husbands,' Peter went on, as Steve lugged a peripheral chair nearer the big desk, leaning back and putting his fingertips together. The elderly gesture made Phyllida wonder, as it always did, if Peter would ever look his age; at thirty-five he could have been ten years younger. 'Coming in together to tell me they'd both lost their wives.'

'Not from natural causes,' Steve said in a dramatic whisper, his pale, sharp-featured face flushing with relish. 'Or they'd have gone to an undertaker. A long time since we had a murder. And two!'

'Not murder!' Peter said quellingly. 'At least, I hope not. The husbands came to report their wives' disappearance while on holiday at the Fountains Hotel. On their own, the husbands hadn't come with them. They checked in on Monday, and when one of the husbands rang the hotel on Wednesday evening to see how they were making out he was told they hadn't returned from a car trip, even though they'd ordered dinner. The husbands did a bit of looking and asking around, and found the car of one of them—the car the women had gone on holiday in—parked at Seaminster station. Locked, but the husband had a spare key and when they opened it it was empty of all but an unbroached picnic basket in the boot. So they then went to the police, and you both know what came next, don't you? As there was no indication of foul play the police could only tell them that adult people have a right to disappear and there was no action they could take. Some of the station staff recognized the photographs the husbands showed them, but that didn't help much because the women used Seaminster station on their not infrequent trips to London. That left recourse to a private investigator, and they found us in the Yellow Pages. Rang just after you'd all gone last night'

'Were the husbands on good terms with their wives?' Phyllida asked.

'They say so, and they seemed genuinely distracted. One—Frank Trenchard—was more extrovert and macho than the other—Matthew Hargreaves—and did most of the talking. The quieter one looked anguished and very sad, but was less openly agitated.'

'You never know how shock is going to affect people,' Steve contributed, with a knowledgeable air.

'And you don't know what people are really like, when you only meet them after their lives have been blown apart, that's one of the problems in this job.'

'Had they any theories?' Steve asked.

'No. They seemed totally bewildered. They and their wives are a friendly foursome, they told me, see each other regularly and have holidays *à quatre*. The week's holiday for the women in Seaminster was mainly to give one wife a break from looking after a mentally and physically handicapped son who lives at home—he's in care for a week—and the other went along for the ride and with the idea of getting some fresh artistic inspiration. She designs book jackets. Both couples live in Appleton, that's a village about ten miles inland from Seaminster just off the London road.'

'Rather close to home to go for a holiday,' Phyllida suggested.

'The book-jacket lady's daughter has just moved in with her boyfriend here,' Peter told them. 'According to her husband—the introvert—the daughter suggested they come here for their little trip and the mother was so thrilled to be wanted that Seaminster is where they ended up. Apparently the daughter had made the booking for them, and they had dinner with her and her boyfriend on Tuesday night. They'd checked in at the hotel on Monday afternoon, as I said, and according to the daughter were very pleased with it, had had a good dinner there on the Monday night. While they were with the daughter and boyfriend they announced their intention of driving into the countryside the next day—Wednesday—and the hotel staff confirmed to the husbands that they'd seen them leave round about eleven-thirty. Unfortunately they gave no clue to anyone as to where they were going, and that appears to be the last time anyone saw them.'

'And it's Friday today.' Steve's relish was returning. 'So they've either done a bunk or they're in trouble.'

'I think we'd agree with that, Steve,' Peter responded gravely. 'To continue. I told Trenchard and Hargreaves as gently as I could that if the worst came to the worst the police would want to know their movements on the day of their wives' disappearance, and they told me readily enough: the quiet one was at home with a migraine in the morning and got to his office—he's an architect—in Lewes at about two-thirty. The other owns a garage in Haywards Heath and told me he took a new Jag for a long test drive in the morning, then came and went in the afternoon. So *if* we discover there's been foul play'—Peter gave Steve a severe glance from which Steve looked airily away—'they neither of them have anything that can be called an alibi. They spent the evening together at a fund-raising evening in Appleton where their wives would have been too if they'd been at home—well, the wife without the tie of the boy, at least.'

'Did they appear to think it possible their wives could have decided to disappear?' Phyllida asked.

'Hargreaves said he wished he *could* think that, it was less awful than the other possibilities, and Trenchard said amen to it. But neither of them seemed able to believe it. Trenchard has the added worry, by the way, that his wife has a heart complaint and isn't supposed to do anything strenuous, or get worked up.'

'Oh, Peter,' Phyllida said, and for the first time Steve looked shocked.

'When I asked them if they could think of anything which might help, Trenchard said reluctantly that both wives had mentioned two men at the art class they, go to together once a week in Seaminster who were always trying to chat them up, and I think it was at that point that both men said how confident they were that their wives would never cheat on them. They couldn't tell us anything about the two men, not even their names, so that I think is your starting point, Phyllida. The women were due at their class on Thursday night, by the way, and they were certainly intending to go because they'd both remarked to their husbands how handy it was going to be, being on the spot. They didn't turn up, need I say? The husbands left photographs of them.' Peter indicated the folder, and Phyllida opened it and took out two coloured snapshots, each of a woman full-length and in close-up. One was tall and sensuously pretty with a lot of wavy red-gold hair, and wore a white, short-sleeved blouse over a long full skirt.

'Maggie Trenchard,' Peter said, 'The ultra-feminine wife with the weak heart who goes with the ultra-masculine husband.'

The other woman appeared shorter and slighter, and had a neat cap of dark hair and small regular features. She wore narrow, navy trousers and a dark jersey with a knotted scarf.

'Carol Hargreaves,' Peter told them. 'The more forceful of the two, I gathered, but that could be something to do with Maggie Trenchard's health.'

Both women looked relaxed and were half smiling. Steve whistled as he looked at Mrs Trenchard. 'Hope they're good likenesses!' he said.

'So do I,' Peter agreed. 'It'll make your job easier. I want you to show them round locally and exhaustively, starting with travel agencies and going on to public places like shops and pubs. And starting now. When you've done all you feel is humanly possible on the spot you can go to London and ask round at Victoria. But I'll want your local report first.'

'Anything, Frank? Anything?' Sally Hargreaves begged on the Trenchard doorstep.

Frank Trenchard shook his head in silence. Through the open door behind him came a quiet male voice interspersed by cooing noises. 'I thought I'd bring Ross home for the day,' he said, 'when Dan said he was free to join us. And you're so good with him too, Sally.'

'I think we'll all be glad to have Ross with us,' Sally said, and Matthew and Jeremy made acquiescent murmurs.

'Come in, come in!' Frank said, into the sudden anguished pause. 'What am I thinking of? I'm pretty glad to see you.'

'We thought . . .' Matthew said quietly as Frank led the way into the sitting-room. 'We thought that as there's only one thing in any of our minds at the moment we might feel better together.'

'I agree.' Frank looked at Sally's laden arms. 'Sally! Thank you for bringing lunch. I should have told you brother Dan would be here.'

'There's more than enough for him. It's untraditional,' Sally said. 'A casserole. But casseroles are the best travellers. Can I stick it in the oven?'

'Sure. I think it's the same as yours.' Frank hesitated. 'Maggie and Carol bought them together.'

Sally felt hysteria rising and whirled out of the room so that she could fight it unseen. Except by Jeremy, who immediately followed her. In the kitchen she nudged a place for the casserole on the crowded draining-board, switched on the familiar oven, and turned, gasping, into his arms.

'It'll be all right,' he murmured at last, stroking her hair. 'You'll see. Meanwhile you've got to hold up. For your father and Frank as well as for yourself.'

'Don't worry. I'm okay now.' Sally drew away from him, blew her nose, ran her hands through her hair, and smiled. 'See!'

'That's more like it. We'd better join them.'

'Yes. Jeremy ... How good d'you think this private detective can be?'

'I don't know. He's got a good reputation. But he doesn't have the resources the police have and he can't go anywhere officially.'

'No. If he doesn't get anywhere the police will *have* to come in eventually, won't they?'

'No. Not unless ...' As she moaned he took her in his arms again.

'Oh, God, Jeremy,' Sally murmured. 'I'm in a nightmare all the time. All day as well as all night. This can't be happening.'

'What's also happening is that I love you.'

'I love you, too.' Most of all at that moment, Sally realised, because he was so comfortingly familiar. When she had been younger, when eros had been no more than a concept, she had seen it as the delicious shock of the strange, she had never imagined it residing in the familiar, the best of the everyday. And it *was* strange, too, of course, at certain moments, those moments which always lay ahead, when it turned both her and Jeremy into unfamiliar driven beings ...

Sally pulled away from him, to check her untimely sensations.

'How long will the oven take?' he asked her, grinning.

'Not long enough. And I want to talk to Ross.'

'Let's hope Frank's doing the drinks.'

'He'll have seen to himself and Daddy, Frank likes his drinks. More than Daddy, I'd say, although Daddy likes his, too.' Sally looked seriously into Jeremy's attentive face. 'The three of us are going to have to be careful about drinks, aren't we? You'll have noticed that I've asked for two each evening since—since my mother and Maggie went missing.'

'I make the second one rather small.'

'I thought so. Come on.' Sally took his hand and drew him across the hall and into the sitting-room, where she ran across the room to Ross's chair and squatted on the carpet beside Daniel, who gave her a smile as he yielded place to her. 'Ross?' she coaxed.

The large rolling head paused just long enough for her to catch the deep-set swivelling eyes, and the heavy lips managed the parody of a smile. 'E-o!'

'He's always pleased to see you, Sally,' Frank said. 'He never forgets you.'

'D'you think he's pleased to be home?'

'You can't tell,' Frank said sadly. 'In a way I have to hope it doesn't make much difference to him. In case ... in case Maggie ... doesn't come back. I'll tell you,' Frank went on in a burst, dropping heavily into a chair. 'I can't help wondering. Did she feel ... did she just feel she couldn't manage Ross any more?'

'No, no!' Sally sat back on her heels, still holding one of Ross's restless hands in both of hers. 'She wouldn't do that, she'd tell you, Frank. Mummy said once how grateful Maggie was that you'd always made it clear to her that having Ross at home was her decision, that if she felt she couldn't cope you'd understand—'

'And that would hardly account for *my* wife's absence, would it?' Matthew shouted. Then immediately apologised.

'It's all right, Matt, it's all right. I'm sorry.' Frank got to his feet and laid a hand orchis friend's shoulder before turning to Jeremy. And I'm sorry to be such a neglectful host. Help yourself to what you and Sally want to drink.'

Over the meal, close round the table, they dropped all pretence of being concerned with anything other than the disappearance of Maggie and Carol. Apart from Ross, of course, and the hazards of his feeding were a welcome punctuation to the futile relentlessness of their speculation. Sally had intended asking Frank halfway through the meal if she could take over from him, but he had already declined Daniel's offer, and as she watched him she saw that he was finding the necessity of moment by moment concentration on Ross's wandering and frequently unreceptive mouth a help.

'Tell us again, Sally, tell us in detail,' Matthew begged, when they were all served and there had been no sound for several seconds beyond the chink of cutlery and Frank's murmured encouragement of his son. 'How they were the night they came to dinner.'

She mustn't hesitate. But to Sally's relief Jeremy was there first.

'They seemed fine, full of enthusiasm for their holiday and looking forward to driving around the countryside the next day. I was detained at the office and was late home, just made it to the meal, but I had plenty of opportunity to talk and listen and—well, I don't know them as well as . . . as I hope to get to know them in the future.' Jeremy had faltered, but managed to find a note of defiant optimism which had Sally and the two husbands painfully smiling their appreciation. 'So I'm not really qualified to say if they were the same as they usually are. But Sally thinks they were.'

'Yes,' Sally said quickly. 'They *were* enjoying their holiday, and—and there didn't seem to be anything worrying either of them.'.Oft, *Mum*! 'Dad!' Sally went on, on a reflex of urgency that took her as well as Matthew by surprise. 'Dad, I'm sure they're all right, I'm sure nothing—serious—has happened to them. That we'll hear from them soon.'

'So you think they've *chosen* to walk out on us, Sal? For God's sake . . .'

'No, no! Of course I don't! I don't know what I think.'

'She thinks she can't accept that they might be dead,' Frank said, and buried his head in his hands.

'No, I can't accept it!' Sally glared round the table. 'And none of us must. We've got to go on hoping, believing . . .'

'Perhaps they've been kidnapped?' Jeremy suggested.

At least it would bring the police in,' Frank said angrily. 'This private eye chap doesn't seem to be getting anywhere.'

'He's showing the photos round locally,' Matthew said. 'And he's going to London. And he's put someone on to the two chaps at the art class.'

'But he can't bully them the way the police could, can't ask a member of the hotel staff to come down to the station if he doesn't like the look iii his eye.' Frank's anger took him to his feet and he began circling the table. Daniel slid round to his seat and picked up Ross's spoon. 'I'm sure he'd be fine if we wanted a debt collected, or somebody followed . . .' Frank stopped abruptly beside the seat Daniel had vacated, sat down, and leaned across the table to Matthew. 'Did our wives need following, Matt? Ought we to have put a tail on them? Did they go to meet men?'

'No, no!' Sally heard her shocked voice before she knew she was going to speak. 'I'm sure they didn't. Frank . . . Dad . . . you mustn't think that, I know it's not true. You must know it, you knew them . . .' She choked on a sob.

'Did we, though?' Frank demanded brutally. 'Did we?'

Ross began to cry, wailing sobs that hurt Sally's ears. 'You're upsetting Ross,' she shouted above the din, angry in her turn. 'And you're not doing any good to any of us, Frank. Stop it!'

'Yes, stop it Frank!' Daniel shouted, distracting them because he was always so soft-spoken and relaxed.

'Watch and pray is the order of the day then, Sal?' Frank inquired after another dreadful pause.

To Sally's relief he now spoke calmly. 'Yes! It's all we can do. And Dad, Frank . . . you're welcome with us at any time, for any meal, and if it just gets too much. We both invite you.' Sally had squared it with Jeremy before coming out, from courtesy rather than necessity, she had been confident he would feel as ready as she was herself to offer practical comfort.

'Thanks, Sally, Jeremy.' Frank passed his hand over his face, and Sally thought how hard it must be for someone of his temperament not to be able to take any action. Her father was more used, by his nature, to thinking than doing, although his face as she lovingly studied it betrayed an anguish an intense as Frank's look of frustration. And Frank had the extra worry over Maggie's health.

'Shall we go down to Seaminster this afternoon?' she asked,

trying to make it sound casual, as she brought in the lemon meringue pie. 'We can take Ross back and then carry on to the coast . . . It's a nice bright day.'

And have tea or something stronger with us,' said her beloved Jeremy without a pause. Sally squeezed his hand. 'When we've walked by the sea. And . . . you'd like to look into the hotel again, wouldn't you?'

'Yes,' Matthew muttered, dropping his eyes to the table. 'Thanks.'

Everyone except Ross joined in the washing up and putting away, so that they could get-off as soon as possible. At least, with someone as alienated as Ross, there was only a one-sided pain at parting, and they left him in his chair in the nursing home's reception, babbling to the receptionist he recognised and unaware of their departure. For a brief moment of which she was instantly ashamed, Sally envied him.

They dropped Daniel off at the little house on the edge of town where he had lived since his wife died, and drove on into Seaminster. The end of March was mild and still after a violent start, and it was blue and gold and beautiful beside the sea, where they strolled the promenade in a leisurely crowd of people and dogs. Since coming to work in Seaminster library after her last exams a couple of years ago, Sally had envied without shame the people whose houses were in sight of the sea. Now, at Jeremy's, she could see it from the sitting-room in the third floor flat, and Jeremy had started talking about buying a house where they would be able to see it from all the front windows.

Sally pulled herself painfully back to the present, noticing that Frank was continually a step or two ahead, finding it hard to keep to the prevailing slow pace of the people around them who were simply enjoying a sunny Sunday afternoon. When they reached the Fountains Hotel he led the way up the steps.

Reception was empty except for a slight, dark young man in a scruffy mac leaning idly against the counter and chatting up the pretty young woman behind it. Sally jerked with surprise as, turning to survey them, he came sharply to a wary attention, relapsing so quickly into his lazy sprawl she immediately decided she had imagined it.

This receptionist didn't know them, and they had to say who they were. 'I'm very sorry,' she responded, shocked. Then brightened. 'But this young man's looking into it and I'm sure—' The girl's hand flew to her mouth as Steve leaned over the counter to put his face close to hers, shaking his head.

'Peter Piper Detective Agency,' he then said reluctantly, turning round.

'Oh, but ...' Jeremy exclaimed in surprise, then stopped, embarrassed.

'It's the name of the firm,' Steve said curtly. He tended to be pleased with himself most of the time, but he knew he didn't have his boss's presence. 'We're doing all we can.'

'And you've discovered ...' Frank's voice cracked.

'Dr Piper will keep you informed,' Steve said, still terse. It wasn't his place to tell them where he was at and he shouldn't be talking to them at all without his boss's sanction. To say nothing of not being in a position to hand them one of the cards he had recently had printed with his name, home telephone number, and the sobriquet *Private Detective*. He hadn't, in fact, handed it to anyone so far, being uneasily certain Peter would disapprove. But he had had the cards done more to impress any likely girls he met than to promote his talents, and at least the half dozen of them he carried about with him felt good in his wallet. 'We have things in hand,' he went on, his restraint making him feel virtuous. And he couldn't be blamed for the girl's loose tongue.

'Have things in hand!' Frank said scornfully, lagging now as they went back to the promenade.

'I'm sure they have,' Sally said, squeezing his arm. Apart from whatever the girl was saying. Didn't you notice? That lad recognised us before we spoke but didn't let on. He was going to listen to us before telling us who he was, make the most of the opportunity fate had thrown him, if the girl hadn't given him away. And he took that philosophically.'

'Why should he want to listen to *us*?' Frank went on angrily, as they began to retrace their steps. Sally noticed that the deep blue of the sea was beginning to fade under the fading sky, but there were still some hardy souls encamped on the sands in the lee of the sea wall. 'We've already talked to his boss, and it's got us nowhere!'

'Some clue we might drop without knowing it?' Sally suggested. Something she must not do. 'Come on!' she said, seizing her father's arm and drawing him across the wide pavement towards the road. 'Time for tea. And there might be a message on the answerphone.'

Chapter Four

'The Hargreaves' daughter's a cracker,' Steve reported to Peter and Phyllida the next morning. 'Toffee-nosed boyfriend,' he added, still smarting from the young man's reaction to his reluctant revelation of his generic name.

'At this moment I'm not interested—'

'They were all tortured and jumpy, but nothing out of the way, considering.' Steve paused a moment, a wary look settling over his thin, pale features. 'The idiot girl in Reception gave me away, told them I was investigating the wives' disappearance.'

'Not down to you,' Peter assured him.

'Thanks, Gov.' Steve's interest in detection had begun with repeats of The Sweeney on TV, and the nomenclature had stuck. And that isn't the real Sunday afternoon news.' Steve paused again, this time for the dramatic effect he sought wherever he could.

'No?' Phyllida supplied.

'No. I went back to the hotel when the bar opened and talked to the barman. He was on duty last Monday, and the two women went in for drinks before their evening meal. He knew at the time who they were because they asked him to put the drinks on their bill and so had to give a room number. And he'd have known anyway by now because of the fuss on Wednesday night when they didn't come back for their dinner and one of the husbands rang. There's more.'

'Yes?' Phyllida prompted.

'He told me that on Tuesday night a couple of men came in—fortyish, slightly scruffy—and asked him if Mrs Hargreaves and Mrs Trenchard had used the bar the night before.' Steve consulted his notebook, a gesture which both Peter and Phyllida knew to be no more than his assurance to them that he had not relied solely on his remarkable memory. 'He said he told them they might have done, and they sat at the counter through a couple of beers apiece looking more and more uncomfy—that was his phrase, he's gay, I'd say—and then wandered off looking disappointed. That was the night the women were dining with the daughter and boyfriend so they were out of luck. Think they might have been the couple from the art class?'

'It's a possibility. Well done, Steve.' Peter turned to Phyllida. 'This makes Thursday's art class important, and we must get photographs. It can't be you in the dark, Phyllida, however ingenious you were the flash would be a giveaway. So it's you, Steve, in daylight, when Miss Moon's identified them.'

'Right. Will you be Lauren Bacall?' Steve asked Phyllida wistfully.

'I don't know yet. I'll tell you tomorrow.'

It was when she started thinking about her art class persona that evening that Phyllida realised how long it was since she had added a new character to her regular cast. Husky-voiced American sophisticate, self-effacing little old lady, large-hearted tart, old-style daily help, head-scarfed market researcher, Home Counties dimwit rushing without insight where more sensitive souls feared to tread, with variations and changes of name they had been her staple characters since the start of her work for the Agency.

Plus the woman who was the farthest from caricature: the laconic Scots lady of her own age whose only constants were her ironic commonsense and her Edinburgh accent.

Her second realisation came with a mingling of disappointment and apprehension. Looking at the role awaiting her now, she had regretfully to admit this was not the moment for a newcomer: the Scotswoman was tailor-made for the part of student on an adult education class in Painting and Drawing. The apprehension came from the fact that the character presented her with difficulties in the playing of her which so far in her cast list were unique: the Scotswoman was so close to her own outlook on life that it required constant vigilance on Phyllida's part not to blur the bounds that separated them and distract herself with envy of the charisma she was convinced she was unable to generate on her own behalf. Perhaps that explained her wistful enjoyment in creating her: this time she overlaid her own sallow complexion with lightly freckled pallor and her own wan hair with a wavy red-gold wig.

Late March was not a good time to attempt to join an adult education class which had begun the previous September, but Peter had managed to tweak one strand among the many that made up what he called his HUN—his Highly Useful Network. To his occasional drinking partner, the deputy director of Seaminster's Arts and Leisure Department, he had spun the tale of a lady (staying, of course, at the Golden Lion), whom his mother had recommended to the coast for convalescence after a serious but unspecified illness, with the plea that she be given a place for the remaining weeks of term on the Department's art class for adults currently in being at the local leisure complex. The deputy director had heeded the plea, while maximising the favour by pointing out that the class had a good teacher and was very popular, being in fact year by year fully subscribed and nearly always fully attended. Their piece of luck—Peter believed that in every case a piece of luck was somewhere embedded—was that the Seaminster Arts and Leisure Department was small enough for there to be only one evening class in Painting and Drawing.

So Jan Elliot, the teacher, was expecting Mrs Steele and had been told something of her recent history. Arriving a courteous ten minutes early from her transformation at the Golden Lion, Phyllida felt personally invulnerable inside her creation and was apprehensive in a purely professional way, the way she was apprehensive when she stepped on stage, and it was a relief when Mrs Elliot offered the instant reassurance of a good co-player. The artist of popular imagination—prominent, Pre-Raphaelite features, straight-fringed black hair and long smock—she floated at once towards Phyllida with arms histrionically outstretched.

'Mrs Steele! Welcome to my Thursday evenings! Your visit to us must be *meant*, you know, because two of our ladies will for the second time be unavoidably absent. It's *very* rare to have an absentee

34

at our Thursday evenings, so the coincidence of your arrival is *quite striking.*'

The long pale hand was cool and dry, with a firm pressure, the large brown eyes were afire with enthusiasm and held no shock or bewilderment. Matthew Hargreaves and Frank Trenchard were so far managing to keep the mystery surrounding their wives' disappearance out of the public domain, as Peter had advised.

'Thank you,' Mrs Steele responded in her soft Edinburgh voice. 'I've been extremely fortunate.'

'We too, I'm sure.' But the tiniest frown had appeared below the fringe. 'Do you ... have you painted and drawn before, Mrs Steele?'

'Not for a long time,' Phyllida said truthfully. She had had a flair for drawing at school, and in the early part of her travelling theatre years had tended to go out with sketchpad and a few watercolours to record her temporary surroundings. Buying materials earlier in the day had been the first time she had thought about why she had stopped, and pondering during the afternoon she had put it down to the loss of contentment which had so soon followed her marriage. 'I used to sketch and do a little watercolour. Landscape and flowers, and I liked painting cats.' Phyllida chided herself for the sense of sorrow which came with the memories, but that was the danger the Scotswoman presented: too *sympathique* to allow her creator to move quite far enough away from her own reactions.

'Splendid!' Mrs Elliot beamed. Phyllida reckoned she could be anything between forty-five and sixty. 'In our Thursday evenings we have all ranges of experience and ability.' She had lowered her voice on the last word after glancing round the room, which was filling steadily with men and women parking their paraphernalia on desks or beside easels before crossing the room to hang their outer garments on the row of hooks beside the door. 'Students choose what subject and what media they wish,' she went on, in what Phyllida already recognized as her normal vibrant tones. 'But I always arrange a still life for anyone who feels they would like to use it. I'm setting tonight's up now, as you can see ...' Mrs

Elliot turned gracefully towards the table in front of the wall of blackboard, where some citrus fruit, apples and a banana lay artistically in and out of a wicker basket. Propped up behind them was a once-white hinged board, partly obscured by a drape of some lustrous green fabric. Mrs Elliot positioned a carafe half full of a faintly pink liquid between the basket and the backdrop. 'If it attracts you at all . . .' she said, with what Phyllida recognized as a fellow actress's assumed diffidence. 'You can sit at the side there, Mrs Steele,' she went on as, with a smile, Phyllida nodded, 'where there's a desk and no easel, Mrs Hargreaves always works in pastel or watercolour. Unless of course you are intending to work in oils?'

'No, no. I want to draw and use watercolours.' In the carrier bag over her arm Phyllida had a new small paintbox and a pencil case with a range of pencils, a rubber, a pen and some Indian ink, and tried to subdue her sudden eagerness to make use of them as tending towards the unprofessional.

'That's splendid, then. And now let me introduce you to the class.' Mrs Elliot clapped her hands like an old-fashioned school mistress and, looking round, Phyllida saw fourteen people come to attention. 'This is Mrs Steele, who will be with us for the rest of the term. She's in Seaminster to convalesce from a serious illness, so don't let her lift anything heavier than her water jar.' Phyllida approved the touch of humour to defuse a moment that could have been heavy, too. 'She's going to sit in Mrs Hargreaves' place, because there.has been a telephone call to say that once again neither Mrs Hargreaves nor Mrs Trenchard will be with us.'

The reaction was graphic, and supplied one of those moments which Peter had named the AWWs, the moments which made it All Worth While. Most members of the class had turned their heads to spotlight for Phyllida, with what her knowledge interpreted as mock sympathy, two men standing together at the back of the room, each in the process of pulling a long scarf from his neck. Both had already shed anoraks and revealed paint-stained sweaters and faded, unfashionably unfitting jeans. Observing their groans and gestures of disappointment, Phyllida also saw that they fitted the description of the two men given by the barman at the Fountains.

'Very well, then,' Mrs Elliot resumed tolerantly, when she had accorded the charade a few moments to run its course. 'Let us commence. I move round the class,' she said to Phyllida, scarcely lowering her voice, 'student by student, offering help where I am asked for it. Rest assured I will not take your brush or pencil out of your hand, Mrs Steele, and add to your work of art. If need be I'll just do a little illustrative drawing or painting on the side.'

'Thank you, I shall appreciate that. And probably ask you for it. I'm very rusty.'

'Artistic skills are not forgotten, Mrs Steele, as I'm sure you'll discover. Tea and coffee are available from the machine in the corridor when we take our halfway break.' Mrs Elliot was already walking away and Phyllida smiled round on her fellow-students, six men and eight women regarding her either openly or covertly, with the two deprived men making no attempt to hide their interested approval of Mrs Steele.

Phyllida sat down and opened her loose-leaf sketchbook, smoothing her hand over the creamy textured surface of the first sheet and rediscovering the anticipatory excitement of that initial contact. On a surge of unprofessional pleasure she realized that to appear absorbed by the task in hand was part of her current persona, so that for once duty and inclination could run together. And detection would resume prime place during that halfway break . . .

By the time the break arrived, and after a lot of initial rubbing out, Phyllida had sketched Mrs Elliot's arrangement almost to her own and, it appeared, to her teacher's satisfaction and had applied her first touch of colour—the suggestion of pink in the liquid in the carafe.

She had also learned that, although the class was seriously intent on painting and drawing and got on with it, the atmosphere was relaxed and members spoke to the room from time to time, notably a thin wiry man called George who seemed to be the class jester and offered an intermittent rueful commentary on his lack of progress, or sudden unheralded accounts of his latest domestic disaster. Phyllida heard one of the two elderly men ask Mrs Elliot to 'do this bit for me' and a breathlessly enthusiastic account to the teacher of an Italian holiday from two cheerful and ethnically clad young women who had returned only the night before. Beside the long window was a table where two elegant older women sat drawing, together with a man with a white beard and piercing eyes who was restless and seemed unable to move about without creating a maximum sense of disturbance. Phyllida caught his eye a couple of times when she looked lip up from her paper, and found the experience so uncomfortable that from then on she avoided looking in his direction.

'That's nice,' a flat female voice said over her shoulder, when Mrs Elliot had decreed the start of the break and Phyllida was yawning and stretching.

It can't be, it's so long since I held a pencil, but at least I'm having a nice time.' Phyllida heard the amusement in Fiona's voice as she got to her feet and turned round.

'It *is* fun, isn't it?' The woman behind her was probably near Phyllida's age, but something faded in her appearance would probably make men like Phyllida's two subjects see her as older. Her eyes were tired and a tight perm had given no body to her lifeless hair, but she still contrived to radiate enthusiasm.

'May I see what *you've* been doing?' But Phyllida's eyes were across the room, watching her two subjects disappear into the corridor.

'I've a long way to go

'But you've made a good start.' Phyllida wished she could have meant it. The woman's attempt at the still life was fatally uninspired. 'I'd like some coffee,' she went on. 'What about you?'

'Oh, yes. I'll show you.'

The reaction of the two men as they met in the doorway confirmed to Phyllida that Mrs Steele would have no need to court their attention.

'Think you'll like it here?' one of them asked as she and her companion brought their paper cups back into the studio. They had stationed themselves in front of the open door so that the women must meet them face to face.

'I do.' Mrs Steele smiled the smile Phyllida always warmed to when she saw it in her cheval glass. 'It's lovely to be drawing again.'

'You gave it up for a while, then?' asked the other.

Their voices and their style were so alike it had taken a longer look to observe that one was fair with a round, full-lipped face and blunt features, the other dark with a sharp nose and narrow mouth.

'I haven't drawn or painted for years. I—'

'Don't listen to a thing these two say!' warned a more powerful male voice from behind her, as with a petulant little moue Phyllida's excluded female companion drifted slowly away towards her seat.

Phyllida turned round. 'Really?' she responded sedately, widening her eyes at a large, cheerful-looking man with a rosy face and a lot of dark wavy hair.

'Really. They're the devoted slaves of two ladies who are away at the moment so they're not free to offer devotion elsewhere.' The man's face was serious, but his eyes danced. 'Actually,' he went on, 'I'd thought Carol and Maggie might be back tonight.'

There was a questioning lift to the end of the sentence, which, after a quick glance at one another, the pair answered with exaggerated shrugs.

'Ah well, better luck next week. I'm Jack Pusey,' the man said, turning back to Fiona and holding out a large hand which Phyllida found drily warm and enveloping. 'And these lads are Des Wilkins and Gary Jones.' Gary was the fair one, Des the dark. 'They're all right, really. You're . . .? I'm sorry, I don't remember what Mrs E said.'

'Fiona Steele.'

'So how d'you like Seaminster, Fiona?' Des Wilkins asked.

'I like it. I always like to be by the sea.'

'Are you staying with friends?' This from Gary.

'I'm staying in a hotel'

Despite the direct questions a wary respectfulness was apparent, and even if Mrs Elliot hadn't interrupted the exchange by clapping her hands again Phyllida suspected the men would have baulked at asking her to name the hotel. As it was, Jack Pusey said he hoped she would enjoy her time with the class, and after a glance at their work in progress Phyllida went back to her place. Jack was working in pastel, rather well, on a snapshot of a dog of many breeds, and while, rather as Phyllida expected, Des was copying a predominantly blue and green calendar photograph of wooded mountain scenery in unsubtly faithful oils, to her surprise Gary Jones was on the finishing stages of a fine delicate watercolour of Seaminster's seafront buildings which if she had seen it in an exhibition or a shop window she would have been tempted to buy.

Back at their places, the members of the class instantly resumed work. For Phyllida, the second half of the evening was tinged with a valedictory glow, as her personal regret swamped her professional relief that her performance had so promptly paid off; Peter's reaction to her report would surely be to decide that Fiona Steele had done as much as she could. He would telephone the deputy director of Seaminster's Arts and Leisure Department, and Fiona would join the lengthening list of women who had been unavoidably called away. And her demise would also be the demise of Phyllida's tutored return to watercolour, leaving her with no more than the hope that her one evening in the classroom would be enough to persuade her not to put her sketchpad and paintbox away, especially now that she could take them to the sea . . .

No! Phyllida corrected herself with the familiar mingling of pleasure and apprehension, She would have to stay around for the possibility—the probability—of an invitation to a post-class drink, which would hardly be issued that night.

But it came as she was collecting her coat.

'We're going for a drink, Fiona,' Gary said, elaborately casual. 'Des and Jack and I. Care to join us?'

To be totally in character Fiona Steele would, the first time, have made an excuse. But, as taught by Peter, Phyllida must always work on the pessimistic assumption that there might not be a second time. Smiling at Jack, Fiona said she appreciated being made so welcome and that it would be very nice to spend a quarter of an hour with them on her way home. 'No more, I'm afraid, I'm expecting a telephone call and I must be back at my hotel by ten.'

It was inevitable now, of course, that within a few moments of their arrival at the Falcon in Jack's car—they told her they took it in turn to drive to and from the class—Fiona's hotel had been identified as The Golden Lion. But thanks to her possession of a room there this was no cause for alarm: once inside, Phyllida need never again emerge as the woman who had gone in. And unless she learned something during the next half hour which indicated that she should continue to attend the class, she probably never would.

'I'm sorry your lady loves have deserted you,' Fiona said demurely as she sipped her wine. 'What is the counter attraction?'

Des and Gary pouted in silence and it was Jack who answered. 'Nobody knows. Apparently one of their husbands rang just before last week's class to say both their wives had gone away unexpectedly and didn't know when they'd be back.' He looked quizzically from Des to Gary. 'There's been some rather wild speculation,' he went on, breaking into a grin as they stared defiantly back at him. 'Perhaps the more so because the ladies had told us during the coffee break the week before last that they were coming to Seaminster for a holiday and would be able to walk to last week's class. They were staying at the Fountains Hotel from Monday to Monday, they said, but as it's turned out they can only have been there three nights at the most, seeing that they weren't in Seaminster for the class last Thursday.'

'Mysterious,' Fiona commented, looking from Des to Gary.

The simultaneous shrug.

'Probably not,' Jack said. 'But whether or no, I suspect it's time these two lads found wives of their own.'

Phyllida saw Des's thin lips tighten and Gary's pink complexion flood red, and decided it was their respect for Jack Pusey that had checked any stronger protest.

'We've been married,' Des told her casually, hiding the defensiveness which had to be behind the information.

'Oh, yes, we've tried it,' Gary added, emboldened. Phyllida realised that Des was the leader. And realized, as the conversation turned to other things, predominantly Mrs Steele and her reactions to Seaminster, that she had obtained all she was going to get.

'I must go now,' she said regretfully, as she drained her glass of wine. 'Thank you all so much for inviting me, I've enjoyed it.'

'We'll run you back to the hotel.' Jack got to his feet.

'No, no!' Phyllida got to hers. 'It's a beautiful night and I've been told to walk. Seaminster's safe and anyway I don't have to go down any side streets. Really, I'd like to walk.'

Three men were no company so far as Gary and Des were concerned, and they nodded. But Jack said firmly, 'So of course you must do so, but you're not walking off into the dark unescorted. I'll see you in a few moments, boys.'

'Here's to more merry meetings!' Gary raised his second pint and Des's hard stare, which Fiona neutralised with a smile, would have embarrassed Phyllida.

'Is Seaminster doing you good?' Jack asked, when they had been walking a few moments and their feet had established a clip-clop rhythm in the crisp silence of the deserted streets.

'I think so. And I like it so much, it has to be.'

'Perhaps you'll come again.'

'Perhaps.'

'Des and Gary,' he said, as they entered Dawlish Square. 'They're all right, you know.'

'You're sorry for them, aren't you?' *Because you yourself are so happily married*? It was Phyllida who asked the second question.

Jack Pusey turned to her in the first sharp gesture she had seen him make. 'Am I? If you're right I'm being horribly arrogant.'

'And I'm being horribly arrogant for asking such an impertinent question.' Phyllida was relieved to hear the irony in Fiona's voice. 'I'm sorry.'

'Don't be, you've given me something to think about.'

As they stopped on the steps of the hotel Phyllida noted with pleasure that the Agency windows were alight. Peter was anxious to hear about the class and had said he'd try to hang on for a chat. As always, Phyllida welcomed the chance to share her impressions while they were fresh. And tonight, as well, she didn't want to be instantly alone.

'I'll see you next Thursday, Fiona.'

'I look forward to it.'

As she watched him walk slowly away, Phyllida was aware that she really would have looked forward to seeing Jack Pusey again.

Chapter Five

'Can I help you?'

From her first day of promotion to senior librarian in the lending section of Seaminster Library, Sally Hargreaves had enjoyed asking that question across her central desk, but now she was desperately grateful for it. While the steady stream of readers responded with their own questions, forcing her to think about the answers or bring them up on her computer screen, she had respite from the turmoil of fear and sorrow churning relentlessly in her head.

From the sense of nightmare disbelief that at one moment even had her pinching her thigh in the hope that she was dreaming and would be able to wake herself up.

It couldn't be real, it couldn't. What she had found out couldn't be true, and what had happened afterwards couldn't have happened. If she went to her old home that evening her mother would open the door to her and take her in her arms . . .

Can I help you?

'Well, I do hope so,' an old lady was responding tentatively. 'I'm afraid it's a rather obscure request, but I'm wondering if you have any books by Ouida?'

'I'm sorry?' Sally queried gently. The old lady's face was thin and pale under the enormous mushroom of her hat, and Sally suspected that the hands inside the beige woollen gloves were clutching at the counter where they rested. 'By whom, did you say?'

'Ouida. I'm afraid it's a difficult name,' the old lady went on apologetically. 'Well, pen name. Ouida's real name was Marie Louise de la Ramée, so I'm not sure how she would appear on your little screen. If she's there at all, of course. Oh, dear, I'm sorry to be such a nuisance. I find it a bit difficult these days to bend down, and when I put my head back I sometimes—'

'Of course. That's all right.' Compassion made Sally cut the old lady's discourse short. 'Hold on just a minute and I'll be able to tell you exactly . . . D'you think you could spell the pen name for me?'

The old lady had a nice smile, and it made her look a great deal younger. 'O-U-I-D-A.' she spelled out, in the soft, breathy, slightly pedantic voice which had revealed at once to Sally that she was well-educated. 'I believe it is what she called herself as a child, unable to pronounce the name Louise. She was a popular novelist in Victorian times although she fell out of favour and these days isn't read at all.' A wistful note was now apparent. 'When I was young I found her books quite wonderfully romantic and now I'm old I just have a mind . . . Is there any chance you might have one or two of her novels? *Under Two Flags* was once, I think, the best known. And there is *Moths*.' Phyllida, in the library earlier in the day in her own persona, had found them both on the shelves.

'Right. Just let me have a look . . .' Sally punched a few keys, then looked up from the video screen in triumph. 'She's here! And so are the two books you mentioned, plus'—Sally peered back at the screen—'one called *Folle-Farine*.'

'Which Bulwer-Lytton considered a triumph of modern English fiction,' Phyllida responded on a reflex, then reflected that it would serve her right if, as their acquaintance progressed, Sally Hargreaves assumed Miss Pym's possession of a similarly detailed knowledge in other literary directions.

'Really?' Sally said politely, wondering who Bulwer-Lytton might be but feeling too weary and uninterested to enquire. And someone else was waiting. 'Look,' she flashed a quick apologetic smile at the couple standing beside the old lady, 'I'll come along with you to see if one at least of the books is on the shelves. If none of them are, you can order . . .' She was already through the flap of her desk, and leading the way to a nearby stack. If the shelf she was making for had been further away she would have called one of the mobile librarians but it would only take a moment. 'They should be here . . . Ah, yes, here's *Moths*. And—'

'Oh, *Moths* will do beautifully!' Soundlessly clapping her gloved hands, the old lady lost her handbag. Sally retrieved it from the floor and handed it back, together with the fat, shabby volume she had taken from the shelf. 'Do you think . . .' Now the pinched white face was anxious. 'Do you think I might sit and read here? It's so nice and warm and the light's so good.' There wasn't the choice of tables and chairs there was upstairs in the reference section where Phyllida sat when researching her book on women and the theatre, but there were a few small round tables with chairs drawn up to them, one only a few feet from Sally's desk.

'Of course! We're open till five and you're very welcome!' The girl was even indicating the place Phyllida had already earmarked.

'Thank you, you're very kind. And now you must go back to your other customers.' And Miss Pym must maintain the good impression she had obviously created, and not become associated in the girl's mind with the prospect of a tedious interruption to the flow of her clientele.

'Enjoy your read, Mrs . . .?' Somewhere the far side of her nightmare, Sally found herself admitting the old lady to her small circle of Named Readers,

'Pym. Miss Agnes Pym.'

Miss Pym trotted over to the table the librarian had indicated and sat down facing the large central desk, and as she opened her hook Phyllida smiled to herself at her choice of Ouida. She'd come across *Moths* in her early teens, and like Miss Pym (and keeping it secret from her contemporaries), had found it romantically engrossing. Over twenty-odd years she had once or twice wondered, idly, how a second reading would strike her, and so when Miss Pym had needed a reason to approach Sally Hargreaves she had looked for Ouida after regretfully abandoning her original idea of carrying on working on her own account. During this series of visits to Seaminster library her subject of study had to be exclusively Sally Hargreaves.

Phyllida had seen her before, and had had Steve's reaction that she was a good-looking young woman. If she had been unaware now of the girl's troubles she might not have noticed the tic at work beside her eye and the slight trembling of her mouth and hands. By the end of the afternoon Sally had proved to Phyllida that she possessed the strength to subject her worries to the demands of her job. She would have been helped, of course, Phyllida reflected (after still finding the first few pages of *Moths* enjoyable), by the family's determination to keep their secret.

Which they could continue to do only so long as the women weren't discovered in a situation where the Police would be called in and would open the way for the Press ...

On an involuntary shudder, Phyllida decided there was nothing to learn from Sally's handling of her other readers she hadn't already learned from her handling of Miss Pym. And nothing unexpected to learn from the short periods when Sally had no customers and the opportunity to work on her screen and the papers on her desk:.Phyllida would have added to her file on the case only if the girl had failed to sigh, look into space, once or twice put her head in her hands, and come back in slight disarray from her tea break.

So Miss Pym must go further. Not that afternoon, because Sally should be allowed to welcome the old lady at least once more without anxiety. But soon.

'I'll leave the book in the library, I think,' she said to Sally just before closing time, when there was no one at the desk. 'It's rather heavy and I don't read much at home.'

'Sure.' Even with her terrible preoccupation, the girl was managing to study Miss Pym's face with slightly curious compassion. 'I'll tell you what,' she said. 'I'll pop it under the counter here with your name on a slip of paper, so that if I'm not here when you want it whoever is in my place will give it to you. Miss Pym, you said?'

'Miss Agnes Pym. May I *know your* name?'

'Sally Hargreaves.'

'Well, that's very kind of you, Sally. Very thoughtful. I expect I'll be in to ask for it tomorrow.'

Miss Ida Jones walked her little dog Gemma—a dazzlingly white

West Highland terrier with ear-tips and tail always sharply aloft—along one route every morning and another route every afternoon. Her morning time was invariable at ten, after she had cleaned and tidied the bungalow, and brought her home in time for a mid-morning coffee. Old Mr Templeton, her next-door neighbour but one, had once told her laughingly on the pavement that he had been known to set his watch by her, and Miss Jones had taken this as a compliment. The time of her second walk of the day depended on the onset of darkness—as late as six in April, May and June, retreating to four o'clock by the end of November.

The routes varied, too. In the morning they walked down to the sea—a half-mile gentle slope—and if Miss Jones adjudged conditions to be right (tide out, sands dry, not too cold or windy), they went carefully down the nearest set of steps on to the shore, where Miss Jones let Gemma off the lead. This was not a signal for the dog to go racing joyously into the distance to cavort with other dogs being similarly enfranchised. Gemma was a sedate little creature, and when released never did more than scamper across the odd low rock or kick a small spray of sand behind her with her back legs. If another dog came up to her it usually, to Miss Jones's strongly voiced disapproval, received a body-trembling, if wary, welcome. So if Miss Jones considered conditions to be unsuitable she did not worry about Gemma being deprived of the chance of real exercise. Gemma herself might pause at the top of the usual set of steps and look up questioningly at her mistress, but when Miss Jones said 'No!' and continued along the promenade, she would make no attempt to lag. Anyway, the one place where she did go a little mad occasionally was always available to her: her own back garden, in which Miss Jones would fondly watch her barking at the neighbouring cats when they pulled faces at her from the wall, and tearing round in sudden circles.

The afternoon walk lay away from the town along similar suburban roads to her own, a circular tour which brought Miss Jones and Gemma home via the other end of their road from the one along which they set off.

The one thing both walks had in common was their beginning.

Both started along the shorter stretch of Bluebell Lane (there was, in fact, a fine crop of bluebells in spring around the apple trees in Miss Jones's back garden), and turned left on to a comparatively, but still pleasantly leafy, main road which ended at a large roundabout. Until a year or so ago, two of the roads giving on to the roundabout, those leading to and from the sea, had been the major road, and the road from which Miss Jones and Gemma approached the junction, with its continuation opposite, had been the minor. As traffic increased so did the juggling for position at the crossroads, and there were a couple of minor collisions. Following a serious accident in which someone was killed, it was decided by the local Highways Committee that Something Had To Be Done.

Had it been done a few years earlier, Miss Jones tended to reflect nowadays as she and Gemma arrived at the junction, it would probably have been traffic lights, but current thinking favoured roundabouts with their scope for sops to conservation lobbies, and in the centre of the junction there had appeared almost overnight, courtesy of the techniques perfected through Chelsea Flower Shows and the various garden festivals held in recent years about the country, a magnificent circular garden raised on a low stone wall.

So splendid was the layout—a central wood crowned with conifers and silver birches sloping gently via well-stocked rockeries to a narrow grass verge—that Miss Jones was forced to admire even through her dismay as she decided that a roundabout, while assisting motorists, presented more hazards for pedestrians than a simple four-lane-ends junction, at which she had always been able to see oncoming cars long before they could pose a threat. Now, each time she set off across the top of one of the roads giving on to the roundabout, she felt she was putting her and Gemma's lives at risk, blind as she was to any vehicle coming from the right until it was almost upon them.

At first Miss Jones had contemplated revising her routes, but within a few days she had discovered that if she crossed well short of the arc which now marked the end of the road, she had sufficient visibility not to be forced to scurry knd pull the steady-paced Gemma faster than the dog wished to go.

49

So both of them had settled into the enforced adjustment, freeing Miss Jones to enjoy the seasonal changes maintained on the roundabout. She had even started to feel she had been presented with a new amenity, when to her surprise and annoyance Gemma, as they reached the first of their possible crossing-points, began to misbehave. This in itself was strange enough, but stranger still in the absence of any incentive evident to Miss Jones. As they approached the roundabout Gemma now regularly began to whimper and then, from the moment they positioned themselves on the edge of the pavement and until they were across the road, to pull on her lead in the direction of the roundabout. Once she had done this so strongly she had caused Miss Jones to stumble in mid-crossing and a motorist, circling too fast, had almost run them down.

After a week of this uncharacteristic behaviour Miss Jones took to scooping Gemma up into her arms as they approached the crossing and not putting her down again until they were well clear of the roundabout. Although Gemma wriggled a bit and continued to whimper, Miss Jones decided that this was probably the safest way to cross even if the dog reverted to her normal exemplary conduct.

And at all other times and in all other places Gemma remained her obedient self. Miss Jones could only deduce that something about the roundabout had started to disturb her, and wished she could have climbed the rockery to investigate. But even vandals left roundabouts alone, and there was no way Miss Jones could see herself scrambling towards the wood under the startled gaze of motorists or her own neighbours or—even worse, somehow—being picked out at night by headlights. No, she would just have to put down to the infinitely superior powers of the canine nose over the human, and assume some odour the far side of no man's land that had either beckoned Gemma or offended her sensibilities.

And then one April morning she saw the foxes. The dead one lying in a curve of the road, eviscerated by a motorist, the live one peering out between the trees.

Gemma was frantic, and remembering the noise she always made in the garden when a fox slunk through, Miss Jones was convinced she now knew what had been attracting the dog to the roundabout. She shuddered as she grabbed her and crossed the road even more quickly than usual, imagining how she would have felt had she in fact climbed up the rockery and come face to face with a live fox. All right on television, quite interesting and attractive in fact, like other beasts confined to pictures, but live and face to face ...

And, well, foxes were *vermin*. Miss Jones would have been hard put to it to define what she meant by that word, but it was one her father and mother had brought out on a reflex if anyone mentioned foxes—or rats, or mice—in their hearing. The expression on their faces as they said it had made it synonymous for Miss Jones with something infinitely undesirable. And there was her ever present fear, when she let Gemma out into the garden after dark, that a fox might attack her. Now, with this new lair they had obviously set up so near her home, that danger was increased.

Miss Jones had to force herself to complete her walk to the sea, she was so anxious to voice her complaint, and even though beach conditions were good she walked Gemma past their set of steps.

'If nothing is done to eliminate this nuisance,' she promised the local Cleansing Department at the conclusion of the telephone call she made the moment she got home, 'I shall ring again. I shall continue to ring until action is taken.'

The prospect of further calls from so determined a voice, combined with the simplicity of investigating so small an area, had its effect, and it took the authority only three days to despatch a two-man team. They parked their van near the top of the road from which Miss Jones had told them she approached the roundabout, and crossed with their equipment on foot, feeling rather ridiculously exposed to the gaze of the circling motorists behind them as they clambered up the rockery.

'It's a bloody forest!' one of them panted as they reached the trees and started to push their way through them.

'Bit of a cheat, though, really,' the other responded, as the trees ended soon after they had begun and they emerged into a small central clearing where no attempt at amenity had been made.

There was no sign of foxes but there was evidence that they had disturbed the open ground. The men walked over to the disturbance and stood staring down. One of them kicked at something half showing through the crumbling earth, and the earth fell away.

'Sweet Jesus,' whispered the other. They've found themselves a foodstore.'

When Miss Jones set out at ten for her morning walk she was gratified to see the pest control van. When she arrived back at the roundabout three quarters of an hour later there were other stationary vehicles, some of them police cars parked oil the curves of the roundabout itself, and a number of policemen. The roundabout was surrounded by a yellow cordon, and when Miss Jones reached her crossing she was stopped and questioned.

'A first for you, is it, sir? It's certainly a first for me.'

'What's that, Fred?' Chief Superintendent Maurice Kendrick, gazing round the restricted space in frustrated disbelief, had registered his sergeant's voice but not what it was saying.

DS Wetherhead decided not to lean forward to remove the small leaf adhering to his superior's left ear. 'Murder victims deposited on a roundabout. Obviously killed elsewhere and deposited, sir, even before we've got Forensics' report—no one with a choice could be persuaded on to a roundabout.' Under his chief's hard stare the sergeant paused for further thought. 'Unless they were tied up, helpless. Which would have made a big risk even riskier. Struggling, shouting . . .'

'It could have been some kind of dare. Which these two unfortunates don't look the type to have undertaken. Thank the Lord, Fred, for a maiden lady's disapproval of vermin. If she hadn't rung the council they could have been here for weeks—this blessèd plot was planned to ignore the seasons at least centrally and save on gardening costs and personnel.'

'I think they must have chosen it so as not to leave a trail, sir, rather than in the hope the bodies would decompose before they were found, because they buried the women with their handbags as well as all their clothes.' DS Wetherhead pointed to a couple of filled plastic bags. Though I suppose the choice could as well have been made by panic as by planning.'

'Dear God what a nonsense!' Kendrick glared up at the sky. 'No chance of a lead beyond this wretched circle. And no houses actually overlooking the roundabout, I noticed when I arrived.' Kendrick discovered that his subconscious had taken note of his sergeant's original comment. 'And yes, it's a first for me, too.' He'd been frustrated on many cases, but never before by the total restriction of his investigation to one small piece of ground.

'And no help so far from the vegetation, I'm afraid, sir. Whoever deposited the bodies got to the centre via the small gap used by the council gardeners, and then of course the gardeners used it just now and left in such a panic that they barged—'

'Yes, Fred, yes. But they still had to send me through virgin forest, just in case.' The small leaf had been bothering the DS, and he was relieved to see it fall to the ground as the Chief Superintendent shook his head. The doctor able to tell you anything?'

'He said he thought the dark one had been strangled. He couldn't say anything about Tiow the blonde died without a laboratory look. He seemed bemused, but aren't we all? Not much depth of soil,' Sergeant Wetherhead went on quickly, lowering his eyes to the ground as they met the laser beam of the Chief Superintendent's. 'Which could have been a shock to the murderer because he'd hardly have felt in a position to take the bodies away and find another burial place. But he should have realised before he brought them here that a temporary structure like a roundabout could only be built on stony ground.'

'Thanks for the geology lesson, sergeant. Now, shall we get on?' Normally Kendrick rather enjoyed his sergeant's regular forays into Authorized Version phraseology, but his sense of frustration, almost of farce, was stiffening into anger.

'Of course, sir,' DS Wetherhead said soothingly. 'It was just that Forensics told me before you arrived that the foxes hadn't had to do much digging. Though the handbags were still just covered.

Everything you'd expect to find in a woman's handbag, John Childs said, although they've obviously been gone through as if the murderer was looking for something. Not evidence of identity, because there's a name and address in a pocket diary in one of them. They let me make a note.'

'Good.' Reluctantly Kendrick's eyes followed his sergeant's down to the remains of the two women, cravenly thankful that although the hessian sacking had been removed—by the foxes and Forensics between them—Forensics had left them face down as they had been lying when found. He knew, though, that the one with no spreading hair to shield the visible half of her mutilated features had already furnished him with an image to add to those which on bad nights rose up, since his loss of Miriam, to torment his mind's eye.

'You're ready for us to remove them, sir?' Kendrick had turned his back on the bodies, and a member of the Forensics team, which had done its work and was waiting by the trees, came diffidently forward.

'Yes, yes,' Kendrick responded irritably. 'We're on our way.'

The man coughed, shuffling his feet. 'You're sure you don't want us to—'

'Thank you, Childs, I've seen all I need.'

Kendrick wasn't usually squeamish, but there was something about these two still young and obviously once elegant women half eaten by wild animals in this open yet enclosed space that was making his gorge rise. Normally, following Forensics' okay, he would have had the bodies turned over, looked at them himself from every angle, but this time he wasn't going to. And it wasn't as if there was any real need, he had a team he trusted and he'd have to see the photographs . . .

'Right, Fred, let's be off.' He thought two sets of eyebrows were slightly raised, but it could just have been that he himself was aware of what he hadn't done. 'Come on!'

Descending the rockery was an undignified stumble, which to Kendrick's surprised relief served to restore his sense of humour.

'Risk it was,' he said, as they gained the narrow curve of pavement.

'So let's hope there'll be no copycats.' He was gloomily aware of the crime reporter from the Seaminster Globe standing beside the police car in which he had been driven to the scene. MURDERED WOMEN FOUND ON WOODED ROUNDABOUT! He could already see tomorrow's headline, in the national Press as well.

'Chief Superintendent!' Sandy Dixon described a circle with his arm, his nose wrinkling in the way it did, Kendrick had noted during earlier investigations, when it scented the bizarre. 'Murder on a roundabout?'

In a few moments the body bags would be carried off. No chance, in these absurd circumstances, of disguising the fact. 'Two dead women,' Kendrick answered him, briefly amused by the sudden and rare look of surfeit in Dixon's freckled face.

'Foul play, of course?' Dixon asked, his lean and hungry look reappearing.

'Too early to say.' Kendrick withheld information from the Press on principle as long as he fairly could, unless there was the prospect of their immediate assistance.

'How did you discover them?' Sandy pressed. 'Hard to believe you were simply being conscientious about a couple of missing persons, Superintendent.'

'Council employees were seeing to the planting,' Kendrick offered. It wasn't much of a lie, and he wouldn't have told it if foxes and corpses hadn't been so inflammatory a conjunction. The lupine connection, too, would soon be common knowledge—Dixon was bound to ring the maiden lady's front door bell before the day was out—but the way he was feeling, Kendrick preferred it to emerge via a source other than himself.

'Oh, aye,' Sandy responded, after a sceptical glance towards the immaculate rim of polyanthus.

'Give us a chance,' the sergeant contributed. 'There'll be hard information soon.'

'There'll have to be, won't there?' Sandy concurred, gazing greedily towards the little wood before shaking his head at the yellow ribbon. The peculiar circumstances of the terrain were frustrating for him, too, Kendrick realised on a flash of pleasure, rendering him temporarily harmless, and he decided to leave Mr Dixon to the clinical mercies of the pathologists.

'Better go straight to that address,' he said distastefully as DC Wetherhead pulled away from the inner kerb. He was going to have to direct a nearest and dearest to the mortuary, and he couldn't do that without warning of the role the foxes had played.

Chapter Six

Miss Pym returned to the library that same afternoon, her face lighting up as she saw Sally at the central desk. Phyllida was pleased, too, that the instant Sally noticed the old lady her tense face broke into a smile and her hand reached under the counter.

'How nice to see you again, Miss Pym! Here's your *Moths*, And your seat awaits you.'

'So I see. Thank you, dear. How are you?' In greater disarray, Phyllida thought.

'I'm fine. Fighting a cold though, so better not come too near.'

'That's thoughtful of you, Sally.' And sensible, to offer a commonplace explanation for moist eyes and husky voice.

Phyllida had enhanced Miss Pym's pallor, and was expecting Sally's next comment. '*You* don't look all that fit, Miss Pym. Are you sure you're all right?'

'Oh, yes, dear, with me it's just age. I'm quite tough, you know.'

But when Miss Pym got up a half hour or so later and started towards the desk, she crumpled into a heap on the floor just as Sally looked round from her computer.

Sally tore through her counter, calling as she ran to a young male librarian loading returns on to a trolley, and they carried Miss Pym between them into the staff rest room and laid her on the couch.

'Thanks, Stephen,' Sally said, as they stood looking down at her. Miss Pym had been heavier than either of them had expected, and they were both out of breath. 'I'll call you if I decide she needs a doctor. Will you ask Sandra to take over?'

The young man went off reluctantly, and Miss Pym opened her eyes and attempted to sit up.

'Just relax, now,' Sally ordered, and was offered a weak smile.

'I'm so sorry, dear. For frightening you when there was no need. It's only low blood pressure, which is unusual for someone of my age, but better they tell me than too high. When I was a girl I was a great fainter in school chapel, such a disturbance for everyone ... Look, you need to go back to work.'

'I'm all right for the moment, someone's taken over. Do you need a doctor?'

'Goodness me, no!' The smile this time was a grin. 'But I *would* appreciate just staying here quietly for a few moments. Can you stay with me?'

'Of course.'

When the young man came back ten minutes later Miss Pym and Sally were-in animated conversation.

'I'm sorry,' he interrupted diffidently. 'But there are two men asking to speak to you, Sally. Has to be personal, they won't speak to anyone else.'

Phyllis watched Sally's pale face turn grey as she let the arm of the sofa take her weight.

'Two men ...' But Sally still contrived to turn to Miss Pym and tell her to stay on the couch for as long as she felt she should.

'Well, you know,' Phyllida sat up and put her feet to the floor, 'I'm feeling better by the minute so I think I'll go home to bed. You have to approve of that, Sally.'

A quick smile. 'Yes, of course, if you're really up to it.'

'I really am. So you go off now and see what those men want.'

And I'll go off and telephone Peter, who will telephone your father.

Good for a firm's image, Phyllida reflected as Miss Pym pulled on her gloves, to know there's more trouble for a client in advance of the client giving notice of it, then chided herself for a trivial reaction in the face of tragedy. Because that was what both her sixth and her common sense told her the two men had come to report.

It took Peter the rest of the afternoon to get Detective Chief Superintendent Kendrick on the telephone.

'Dr Piper, I believe?' the remembered deep voice said at last. I'm told it's urgent.'

Under the dry tone Peter thought he detected wariness. Or perhaps it was just that he was expecting it. This was not the first time the DCS had found himself on the receiving end of Peter Piper knowledge and expertise, and on that earlier occasion Peter had not been surprised to recognise that the senior policeman had failed to enjoy the position.

'Well, yes, I rather think so,' Peter said apologetically. 'You see, I've been retained to investigate the disappearance of two women—Carol Hargreaves and Maggie Trenchard.' Peter heard the sharp breath the other end of the line. I've learned this afternoon from my clients that the women—their wives—have been found dead. Possibly murdered. So obviously the case is out of my hands now, but in view of my contacts with the bereaved families . . . My clients approached the police before they approached me,' Peter went on hastily, 'but at that point it was simply a disappearance and they were told that adults have a perfect right to disappear if they choose to. They were on holiday in Seaminster, and the husbands found the car they'd gone in parked at the station here, which seemed to suggest they'd gone off of their own accord. My Miss Bowden'—another sharp breath . . . 'has made the acquaintance of the Hargreaves daughter, though not as herself, you understand . . .'

'I'm sure I do.'

At least the voice, though even drier, was still calm. Kendrick himself, in company with a hundred per cent of Peter Piper clients, had never met Phyllida—known professionally as Miss Mary Bowden—in her own persona, but had encountered sufficient of her various and contrasting manifestations to remain unconvinced, Peter suspected, that the Agency deployed only one female assistant in the field.

'Actually,' he went on swiftly, 'I'd just about reached a point where I was beginning to feel I should approach the police. Although, as I said, Miss Bowden has got to know the daughter of one of the victims, and has identified a couple of men the husbands told me used to chat their wives up at a weekly art class,'—this time the Chief Superintendent coughed—'I'd got nowhere with my investigation and my clients were growing steadily more certain that something serious had happened to their wives. They were unshakeable, you see, in their belief that they would never have chosen to disappear. They were spending a week at the Fountains Hotel, by the way, and drove off into the countryside last Wednesday morning. That's the last anyone saw of them until their bodies were discovered. Matthew Hargreaves was almost incoherent by this time, but I gathered they were in a rather extraordinary—'

'The bodies of Maggie Trenchard and Carol Hargreaves were discovered on the new wooded roundabout just outside Seaminster.' He'd have to get used to saying it. 'Mrs Hargreaves had been strangled and Mrs Trenchard had died naturally. Of heart failure probably, her heart was in poor shape as you obviously know. No doubt you will have learned the rest of it, too, from your clients.' Kendrick had to struggle to keep his feelings of hostility out of his voice. Which he had to do, he was obviously going to need Peter Piper and his Miss Bowdens.

'No. I haven't.' Peter tried not to sound soothing. 'Hargreaves was too cut up to say more than that both wives had been found dead on the roundabout and he'd tell me more when I call at Trenchard's house tonight. If that's still all right by you,' Peter added quickly. 'I've been thinking, Chief Superintendent,' he went on, following Kendrick's curt affirmative. 'Apart from knowing the time had come to liaise with you, as I and my team have done some investigation and maybe turned up some information which could be useful to you, would you like me to come and see you?'

No, I would not! Kendrick responded in his head. But he was a realist, and Piper had to be set in the scale against the sterile circle of the murder scene. The trouble was, he had been feeling angry before Piper's call.

'Yes,' he said. 'Shall we say as soon as you can get to me?' Kendrick hesitated, then decided with relief that it would be neither provocative nor unprofessional to allow himself one small temporary respite. 'On your own in the first instance. I'll see—Miss Bowden—after you and I have talked.'

'A pity your Miss Bowden wasn't around when we broke the news to the bereaved,' the DCS lamented unfairly as Peter sat down in the chair the far side of his desk. But it gave Kendrick a slight sense of retaining the initiative to be the first of them to mention Piper's field chameleons.

'Yes,' Peter readily agreed. 'But no one meets Miss Bowden in her own persona, and so far the closest she's been able to get to the families is as an elderly lady who has recently made the acquaintance of the Hargreaves' daughter, Sally, in Seaminster Library where, as you'll know, Sally works. We were hoping—'

'That the acquaintanceship would ripen into friendship?' Kendrick was a trifle amused to find himself mollified to discover that Miss Bowden was a cypher to everyone.

'Well, yes. As for *now*,' Peter went on eagerly, leaning towards the desk, 'Mr Hargreaves had only just heard the news when I rang to tell him that what looked like two CID men had called on his daughter at the library.' He and Kendrick stared at each other expressionlessly. 'When he told me why he could scarcely get it out, he was still so punch-drunk. So I got to hear his reaction to the news—'

'His apparent reaction,' Kendrick corrected.

'Of course. I got to hear his apparent reaction, if not to see it. I offered to drop everything and go over to his office, but he told me there was a police presence liaising with his secretary to make him tea. And of course, his daughter would be on the way. When I spoke to my other client—Trenchard—he asked me to join him and Hargreaves this evening at his house. He sounded cut up too, as bewildered and unbelieving as the other chap. D'you think—'

'We've no evidence at the moment that points to either of the husbands having had anything to do with their wives' disappearance and death,' Kendrick supplied reluctantly. And on the other hand we have no evidence as yet to prove that they didn't.'

'When Hargreaves and Trenchard first came to me,' Peter ventured tentatively, 'they offered me alibis for the day of their wives' disappearance. Half jokily, but they said they'd had them ready for the police, so I told them they might as well give them to me. Actually, it was more lack of alibi. Hargreaves had apparently spent the morning in bed with a migraine and gone into his office about two-thirty, where he then remained until about half-past five. Trenchard had been test-driving a new car most of the morning, and coming and going in the afternoon. In the evening—when the wives must have been dead but work would probably still have been under way in preparation for the small-hours dumping—they'd gone together to some charity do where their wives—at least the wife without the handicapped son—would have been with them if they hadn't been on holiday.'

'Um.' So Kendrick would have to tell his investigating officers to look out for inconsistencies between two sets of statements, but found himself not wanting Piper to see that he rated his information highly enough to pass it on there and then in his presence. For the time being, though, they had just about finished. 'Thank you, Dr Piper. I suggest you carry out the visit arranged for tonight. On the understanding,' Kendrick continued, becoming all policeman and relieved to note that Piper was aware of it, 'that you faithfully relay to me anything that strikes you as being inconsistent with the natural grief of a husband whose wife has been directly or indirectly done to death by a person or persons as yet unknown. Is that clear to you?'

'Absolutely clear, Chief Superintendent,' Peter responded primly. And coinciding with my own instincts, as I hope you would expect of me. I consider myself privileged to be in a position of perhaps being able to assist the police with their inquiries.' He was relieved to find himself uttering the absurd ambiguity, it enabled him to relieve the portentousness of the atmosphere with a shake of the head and a rueful smile.

To his relief the Chief Superintendent returned the smile. 'I'll be glad to have your up-to-date file, Dr Piper, on everything. Ah.' A folder had been pushed across the desk. Thank you. Now, has Miss

Bowden's acquaintance with Miss Hargreaves reached a point where Miss Bowden can call on the girl at home to offer her condolences? It's unlikely Miss Hargreaves will return to the library for a while, if only in view of media reaction ...'

Kendrick tailed off as each man saw the apprehension in the other's eyes.

'Oh, Lordy!' Peter said at last. 'It's going to be a media field day, it's got everything going for it. Including a roundabout. Cuts off the clues, that, doesn't it?'

'Yes,' Kendrick agreed shortly. 'It does. Dr Piper, has Miss Bowden reached a stage where she can call on Miss Hargreaves?'

'I've only spoken to her on the phone since her visit to the library today, but from what she said I should think yes. And the woman Miss Hargreaves has met is a frail old lady who would be hard put to give offence.'

'A true mistress of disguise, your Miss Bowden.' Kendrick tried to speak lightly. But the more he told himself he must view Miss Bowden as an ally, the more hostile to her he felt.

'She is rather good, yes. It's a gift, isn't it?'

'It must be.' Part of Kendrick longed to question Peter Piper about Miss Bowden, discover her—or their—real age and background or backgrounds, and the other part didn't want to think about her at all. The worst thing, of course, would be to give in to the curious part, and have Piper boom him off. 'What you have agreed to do for me, however, obviously can't be a gift. Dr Piper, I'm authorized to tell you that the police will meet a bill commensurate with the bill you would present to your clients if you were continuing your investigations on their behalf. Is that satisfactory?' Kendrick fell silent, and looked at Peter with stern inquiry.

The offer was tacit proof of the value Kendrick had put on the Agency's help in the past, and Peter had to struggle to keep his sense of gratification out of his face. 'Thank you, Chief Superintendent, that's very fair, and I'm sure I'm speaking for Miss Bowden as well when I accept it.'

'Good.' Kendrick got to his feet. 'I'm grateful for your

co-operation, Dr Piper, as you must realise.' As he himself must realise. 'I suggest you come to see me again in the morning if that's not too difficult. Eleven?'

Peter nodded.

'Thank you. As regards your visit tonight to Trenchard: you're going to his house because of the gravity of the situation, and to tell him and Hargreaves in person that you cannot of course continue your investigations now that the police are on the case. You will also tell them that you have passed on to us your findings—such as they are'—Peter nodded again, in acknowledgement of the small put-down—'about the men at the art class.' Peter answered the half-query in Kendrick's face by nodding towards the folder lying on the desk top between them. 'Thank you. Although you can no longer help them professionally, you wish to assure them both that if they want someone understanding to talk to, ease their grief . . . You get the picture, Dr Piper?' Kendrick inquired, trying to hide his distaste for the scene he was setting. And it was hard to offer the proper sobriquet to a man whose doctorate was in Crime Fiction.

'I do, Chief Superintendent.'

'Good. I ask you, of course, to keep your firm's continuing role in this investigation entirely to yourself and your assistants.'

'That's understood.'

'For my part,' Kendrick went on, trying not to sound grudging, 'I undertake to pass on to you anything the police discover which I believe may assist you and Miss Bowden.' He had a sudden surprising thought. 'If Miss Bowden, in the new circumstances, is prepared to continue her investigations, of course.'

'She is. She's happy to keep the old lady going, and to create any other character who can tread where the Agency as the Agency can't.' *And the police can't*, Peter concluded, but only in his head. 'My clients know that I've traced the two men at the art class, but they don't know how it was done and of course they don't know we're courting Miss Hargreaves.'

'Miss Hargreaves . . .' Kendrick took a deep breath. 'Bring Miss Bowden with you in the morning,' he invited, getting to his feet.

'Who identified the bodies?' Peter asked as he followed suit. 'I can hardly ask the family.'

'The husbands.' Kendrick hesitated. 'It was a particular ordeal, because there were foxes on the roundabout. That's how we found the bodies, because someone reported the foxes. Which probably means they'll be in the news as well tomorrow.'

Trenchard's front door was opened by Matthew Hargreaves. He was smaller and paler than Peter remembered him and had to make an obvious effort to focus his eyes on Peter rather than stare through him, but to Peter's surprise he seemed more in control than the so much tougher looking Frank Trenchard, now slumped in a chair and not looking up as Peter and Hargreaves entered his living room. An elegant room, Peter swiftly noted, more likely owing its charm to the deceased wife than to the surviving husband.

Hargreaves' daughter was also sitting down, but got to her feet when she saw Peter, although he was aware that she was supporting herself against the sofa as she looked at him dull-eyed and without curiosity. Despite her disarray Peter found it easy to see why Steve had found her dark delicacy attractive.

'Here's Dr Piper,' Hargreaves muttered.

There was no response from Trenchard, but the girl said 'Thank you for coming,' and made a small gesture of the hand which Peter turned into an extended arm and a handshake by extending his own. Her hand was very cold, although the room was stuffily warm. 'Please sit down and Daddy will get you a drink.'

Already playing the role of woman of the house, Peter commented to himself, and *it isn't even her parental home*. But Sally Hargreaves had two unmanned males on her hands and he had learned from personal experience that a characteristic of very bad news is that it seems, in the instance of its revelation, to have taken place a long way in the past.

'Thank you.' He took the armchair matching the one where Trenchard was huddled. When Hargreaves had put a whisky into his handle sat down on the sofa beside his daughter.

All three of them were now looking at Peter with a sort of

dreadful pleading which he had to acknowledge. 'This is terrible,' he said, speaking as it came. And I can't even try to do anything more for you, now that the police are in charge. I've told the Chief Superintendent that the Agency has pinpointed the two men at the art class your wives attended, but it's up to them now to talk to them if they think that's indicated.'

'Of course it's bloody indicated!'

Peter had jerked in shock at Trenchard's sudden and explosive entry into the conversation. The man was still deep in his chair, but his head had come up and his bloodshot eyes roved angrily round the room.

'I would agree,' Peter said soothingly.

'It's the only lead we've got,' Matthew Hargreaves said quietly. 'But we mustn't start building on it, Frank. Maggie and Carol could simply have been in the wrong place at the wrong time, the victims of a roving madman.'

'Perhaps if Carol had been shot,' Peter interjected tentatively. 'But strangulation . . .'

'At least we don't have to wonder how or why Maggie died,' Frank muttered.

'I don't think we can bear it, really,' Sally said to Peter, in an explanatory, almost conversational tone.

For the first time in his professional career Peter was actively glad not to be a policeman. He found himself getting to his feet and crossing to the sofa simply to lay his hand for an instant over hers where it twitched on her lap.

'Nothing can lead to a roundabout,' Trenchard muttered, his head now down again on his chest. 'Nothing. Bloody clever. Worth the bloody risk.'

Matthew Hargreaves made a moaning sound, and shuddered the length of his body.

'Have you been . . .' Peter began, then paused, realising with a fresh stab of horror what they were discussing.

'We've been, yes,' Hargreaves whispered. 'Not on to it, although the police had finished and told us to be their guests.' The sound of the two men's laughter was horrible, and Sally cried out in protest. 'There were foxes on it, you know, and they'd . . . That's how they were discovered. A woman walking her dog saw them.'

'So that we were still just able to identify them,' Frank said, raising his head and glaring at them in turn.

Sally cried out again and, retching, Matthew Hargreaves buried his face in a handkerchief.

'Daddy and Frank spared me,' Sally whispered to Peter. 'I didn't have to look at them. Oh, Daddy!'

She threw herself on the floor at her father's feet, and he leaned down and took her into his arms. Peter took a sip of his whisky and tried to believe his presence was continuing to be helpful, because it was hardly the moment to excuse himself.

And when Sally hoisted herself back on to the sofa, slowly and heavily as if her body was weighted with lead, she turned to him and told him she was glad he was there. 'I know you can't work for us any further, Dr Piper, but if we can keep in touch, perhaps talk occasionally . . .'

'The DCS had got it right. 'Of course. My concern for you all hasn't switched off because the police have taken over.'

'Thank you. And thank you for tracing those men at the art class.'

'I've told the police all we discovered about them. Not much, I'm afraid, but at least they know their names.'

'So do we,' Trenchard growled. 'And that they had a drink in the Fountains Hotel the night before Maggie and Carol disappeared.'

'The police know that too,' Peter said reassuringly, seeing a sudden frightening scenario in which a crazed Trenchard went forth in vengeance. 'And it's for them, and them, alone, to discover,' he went on, 'whether or not their interest in your wives was innocent.' He heard the sudden steel in his voice and saw it in the way even Trenchard came to attention.

'Of course,' Matthew Hargreaves said, with an uneasy glance at his friend.

Trenchard reached out for his glass, drained it, and dropped his head.

Peter got to his feet. 'I must leave you now,' he said, in his normal tone. 'But please don't hesitate to get in touch if you want to talk, ask a question . . .'

'We won't,' Hargreaves said. 'Thank you.'

'I'll see you out' Sally Hargreaves got slowly to her feet and plodded to the front door on legs that looked as though they should be dancing.

'I'm so very sorry,' Peter said on the step. 'You'll stay away from work for a while?'

'I'd rather not, but until the media have finished . . . They'll have a field day, won't they?' she asked him, echoing his own fear of what lay ahead.

'I'm afraid so.'

'The police are releasing names tonight, they told us.' Sally looked round the deserted darkness of the Trenchard forecourt and shivered. 'This is the last moment of our privacy, Dr Piper, so I can't go back to work right away although I think I'd like to.'

'You're a realist, Miss Hargreaves.'

'But someone once said that human beings can't bear very much reality. Dr Piper . . .' He saw her hesitate, saw something in her eyes he interpreted as an intrusion into her grief.

'Yes?' What he saw could be impending revelation, and he held his breath.

'No,' she said, on a heavy sigh. 'There's nothing more to say. Just getting from one moment to the next is an achievement, and the worst thing is that I can't imagine it ever being any different. I used to enjoy watching the foxes on the lawn. Goodnight,' she said hurriedly, and ran back inside and closed the door as her tears began.

Peter was truly upset, and intended to accord her grief a brief mental silence. But before he had his seatbelt fastened he found himself visualising the scenario of Miss Pym's visit next morning to the library, and trying to work out how she could explain convincingly to Sally her knowledge of Jeremy Clark's address.

Chapter Seven

The morning after the discovery that they were dead, Maggie Trenchard and Carol Hargreaves became national celebrities. Broadsheet and tabloid alike carried banner headlines, and both the BBC and the commercial TV channels opened their news bulletins with a view of the small board on the edge of Britain's first famous roundabout, announcing its sponsorship by a local firm of funeral directors. Kendrick, to his immediate chagrin, gave a shout of triumph as he watched an early transmission over his solitary breakfast, because he had a bet on with his DS that one at least of the companies would be unable to resist the ironic lead-in.

Phyllida, who had been unaware of the detail, experienced a physical shock which made her spill the mug of tea in her hand. Thinking sorrowfully of Sally she put the outward signs of Miss Pym into a bag and set out on foot into a clear crisp day, cheered despite her sombre mood to discover that as early as nine o'clock the calm sea was already tinged turquoise from a pastel sun.

A thrush was repeating its indignant song as she passed a row of small front gardens, strong enough to prevail over a wheel of crying seagulls turning above the edge of the tide, and a hawthorn hedge was burgeoning a brilliant green. The hedges had been bare and the songbirds silent when she had left her husband and the Independent Theatre Company in which they both worked. Phyllida did not regret her abandonment of either, but the excitement of landing the TV contract and then her job with Peter had somehow got in the way of discovering who she had become via the dying of her marriage and her departure from the theatre, and to her uneasy surprise the characters she was now assuming offstage were more real to her than her own. They were also helping her continue to postpone the self-assessment she was half afraid could lead to the discovery that Phyllida Moon no longer had an identity.

She had, though, done one important thing to help stem the undercurrent of bewilderment which had followed her two adieux: she had bought the house she had rented when she had decided to stay on in Seaminster, and secured the daily solace of the sea. The weather had to be actually dangerous, with water-borne rocks and stones hurtling over the sea-wall, to make her follow an inland route to the Agency.

Love of the sea was Phyllida's link with her Cornish childhood, but walking beside it in Seaminster had so far brought her no nearer self-discovery. Even when she walked for the sake of it the effect was to lead her away from herself—a path she so willingly took—and encourage her to think about new characters or the progress of her book. But this at least she could do only as herself, so that she was regularly reassured Phyllida Moon still had a brain if not a personality ...

Outside the Golden Lion there was an unseasonal jostle of cars, and in the foyer a huddle of men and women who did not look as if they could have afforded the hotel's terms out of their own pockets was struggling for position at Reception. Phyllida exchanged the usual expressionless nod with one of the harassed people behind the desk, crossed the foyer, and climbed the back stairs to the small basic room with bath which was at her permanent disposal. Peter had handed the police details of a sophisticated robbery racket that was threatening to destroy the Golden Lion's unique reputation, and its manager, John Bright, to Peter's surprise if not the surprise of his or John's staff, had felt the agency fee to be inadequate recompense for the salvation of his business.

As always on arrival in what she thought of as her office, Phyllida rang down to ask if there were any messages for any of the women whose names were currently with Reception, and was relieved for once to learn that there were not—as she was feeling, it would have been difficult to share the Hargreaves murder with other concerns.

Miss Pym was so total a transformation, both inside and out, that she was one of Phyllida's most easily assumed characters, and it was not much more than half an hour later when the old lady, looking smaller and slighter than the tall, slender woman who had entered the hotel, trotted across the foyer, this time with a vague, all-embracing smile towards the still embattled receptionists. As she left the hotel Phyllida glanced across Dawlish Square at the Agency windows, but didn't slacken Miss Pym's steady pace until she reached the flight of stone steps up which a small group of men and women wreathed in photographic equipment were surging towards the ornate Victorian porch of the municipal library.

'Excuse me . . . I'm very sorry . . .'

She had timed it well, the heavy oak door was just opening. Miss Pym gave a quavering cry as she apparently fell foul of the metal corner of a camera, loud enough to check its owner, evoke a muttered apology, and be pushed ahead of him up the steps like a hostage so that she escaped being trampled or excluded as the group was forced to narrow in order to negotiate the doorway.

'How very kind . . .' Miss Pym turned for a grateful glance, but her bodyguard was already tearing past her. Content now to take her time, Phyllida let the rest of the crowd go ahead, relaxed once she had ascertained that the young girl sharing the centre of the besieged desk with the young man whose strength she had taxed the day before was not Sally.

But Miss Pym must show her disappointment at Sally's absence as well as bewilderment at finding herself in the centre of an aggressive crowd. She had listened to the news while having her breakfast and been shocked to learn of the local murder without making the connection with the girl who had been so kind to her.

'Sally . . .' she faltered, when the young man helping to hold the siege turned to her with a smile of relief and recognition. 'Stephen—it is Stephen, isn't it?—where's Sally? And who are all these people?'

'Oh, God, you don't know . . .?'

She had been lucky. Unless he had an exceptionally fine sense of priorities, the young man would hardly be keeping his attention on Miss Pym if he hadn't already met her in circumstances, almost as dramatic as this morning's. 'Please wait your turn!'-he said sharply to the media man who was trying to elbow the old lady aside, not taking his sad gaze from her anxious face. 'Look, Sally's mother's been murdered, and this is the media.' He gestured to the surge around her. 'So as you'll appreciate she's not here. Look,' he said again, forced by the determination of the crowd to be aware of it, 'I'm afraid I'll have to—'

'Of course, you mustn't spend time on me this morning. But oh dear ... Stephen!' The sudden sharpness of Miss Pym's tone had reclaimed the young man's attention and he leaned towards her as she sank her voice to a murmur. 'Sally's my friend and I'd be so very grateful for her address. Or her telephone number, except that perhaps she won't be answering the telephone at the moment. Oh, dear ...'

'I don't know ...' His harassed gaze roamed the impatient faces to each side of her.

'I won't give it to anyone else,' Miss Pym whispered conspiratorially. 'Please, Stephen, I must comfort her.'

'Hang on, then.' The young man's head dipped for a moment to the invisible shelf under the hang of the counter, and as he raised it his hand slid a slip of paper under Miss Pym's, lying gloved on the top.

'Oh, thank you!' In one rapid movement Phyllida slid the paper inside the other glove, a precaution Miss Pym's vaguely smiling glance to right and left of her confirmed as unnecessary—with her lack of challenge and charisma, the old lady was turning out to be the best choice she could have made for the woman to gain Sally Hargreaves' confidence. 'I'm so very grateful. And now you must see to your other customers.'

Out in the street Phyllida transferred the slip of paper to Miss Pym's old-fashioned two-handled bag, made her way back to Dawlish Square, and took the gilt-meshed lift rather than the elegant curved staircase up to the Agency's second floor office.

Jenny was at the computer and Steve was lolling against the restroom doorpost. Jenny looked round to smile a welcome, but

Steve regarded Miss Pym in despair and banged his head against the wall.

'Steve?'

'I thought it'd be Anita Sunbury,' Steve muttered.

'Thank heaven it wasn't just now, I could hardly have had Sally Hargreaves's address and telephone number handed to me with half the country's media standing around.'

'You got it!' Jenny breathed admiringly. She looked so pretty with her wide blue eyes, perfect complexion and dark curls that Phyllida marvelled, not for the first time, why it was that Steve didn't see her as a potential date. Or she Steve, for that matter, Phyllida continued to muse, with the paradoxical sense of relaxation and homecoming she was always aware of when she pushed open the agency door. But then Steve, despite his defensive awareness of his masculinity, had been endowed by nature to display it with no more obvious help than a waif-like thinness and a bright eye. Watching Jenny pull a pitying face at him and Steve pass an ungentle hand over the dark curls, Phyllida reflected that it probably made for stability in a workplace when the members of staff saw themselves and each other as older and younger siblings.

'Yes, I got it. I'd expected to have to ask a member of the Press but I was lucky, the young man who helped Sally pick Miss Pym up yesterday was on duty in her place and was more pleased to see her than he was to see the media.' Phyllida looked at her watch. 'Now, I'd have liked the usual coffee but Peter and I are due to attend on Detective Chief Superintendent Kendrick—'

'In a quarter of an hour,' Peter finished, shrugging into a jacket as he appeared at his open office door. 'And I heard the good news. How d'you think of tackling it?' he asked Phyllida, as they approached the gilded doors of the lift. It was on its way up, and after exchanging murmurs of acknowledgement with the occupier of another office suite who emerged from it he made a courtly show of handing Miss Pym inside.

If Peter didn't approve a course of action projected by a member of his staff he said so, but he always began, to Phyllida's approval, by asking the person concerned what his or her ideas were, and sometimes changed his own as result.

'I thought of trying the telephone first, and then I thought that if I was told she didn't want to see anyone that would have to be the end of it. So, if you agree, Miss Pym will simply present herself.'

'I agree. Make it three-thirty, fourish, after she's tried to rest.'

'Great minds, Peter.'

The pattern of the paths across Dawlish Square was outlined by narrow ribbons of soil which the municipal gardeners had set aglow with polyanthus. The early colour of the day had faded and the flowers were so bright under the grey sky they could have been lit from within. 'I wonder who the Chief Superintendent is expecting you to bring with you today,' Phyllida said as they set off along a brilliantly defined diagonal.

'I have an idea he rather likes Mrs Sunbury, so he'll be disappointed.'

But Kendrick's reaction to Miss Pym as she crept apologetically into his office was that she was a stray member of the public who had somehow got past his outer defences, and that for some reason about to be explained to him Dr Piper, a few steps behind her, had again come alone. He had to be grateful to Piper, Kendrick thought wryly, that he put his hand on the old lady's shoulder and introduced her quickly enough to save a very senior policeman from risibly undermining his gravitas.

'Miss Pym. I see. Please sit down.' He had been delivered from one gaffe, but to his annoyance Kendrick found himself moving round his desk to pull his most comfortable chair forward, no doubt demonstrating to Dr Piper and his assistant as well as to himself that his instincts at least were still unable to accept that Miss Bowden was one healthy young field operative.

'Thank you,' Miss Pym said politely, smiling at him from a thin, elderly face in which Kendrick could see no trace of Anita Sunbury. But he was uncomfortably aware of his bewilderment as he conceded the familiarity of the voice that emerged from Piper's other females. Motioning Piper to another chair he went back behind his desk, touching a button as he sat down which brought an immediate

74

tap on the door and a young uniform carrying a tray containing coffee and biscuits. The uniform dispensed both while Kendrick sat in impatient silence, asking Dr Piper as the door closed how he had got on the night before at Trenchard's house.

'Nothing I wouldn't have expected,' Peter told him. 'The three of them appeared to be in total bewilderment and disarray. You were right, about my new role, Chief Superintendent, they asked if they could keep in touch etcetera.'

'Good. Now . . .' Reluctantly, Kendrick glanced at his other visitor, motionless in her chair with her gloved hands in her lap. 'I've read Miss Bowden's report on the two men at the art class the dead women attended, and I have to tell you that they are the same two men who had a drink in the bar of the Fountains Hotel the night before Mrs Hargreaves and Mrs Trenchard went missing. The barman recognized the photographs of them taken by your male operative.' Kendrick was annoyed again to hear the wariness in his voice. So far there had been no indication that Piper's male field worker was a composite, but he realized he was braced for a parallel piece of disturbing information. 'So good work from your staff, Dr Piper.'

'Thank you. I suppose that winds up Mrs Steele's attendance at the art class.'

'On the contrary. New evidence has come to light which indicates that she should continue to attend, if she is willing.' What would not come to light, Kendrick commented grimly to himself, was that the piece of paper which had transformed the case had been overlooked by Forensics in their preliminary examination of the women's clothes, and been discovered only that morning.

And does she take sugar? Phyllida would have asked her interior question crossly if she hadn't been so pleased to learn of Fiona Steele's stay of execution. And the Chief Superintendent's grave gaze was on her at last, inviting her to give her own agreement as she reproved the unprofessional leap of her Jieart at the prospect of at least two more hours with her pencil and brush under tuition. 'Yes,' Phyllida said swiftly, 'I shall be happy to carry on, Chief Superintendent.'

'Good. A piece of paper recovered from a small pocket in Mrs Hargreaves' blouse carried a computer-printed message. It said'—Kendrick looked down at some notes on his desk—"£500 to the usual place on Wednesday, or I tell your husband what you've been up to." What do you think of that, Dr Piper, Miss Pym?'

'I thought it was usually the blackmailer who got killed rather than the victim,' Peter suggested, after a short pause to absorb his surprise.

'The victim could tell the blackmailer that the supply had dried up and she was going to the police. But it's all supposition at the moment and we obviously have to talk to the men at the art class,' Kendrick said. 'I'll be carrying out my own investigations there. If the men witnessed some unorthodox behaviour on the part of Mrs Hargreaves the odds are that they witnessed it before, during, or after the class. So you can see that Miss Bowden's continued attendance will be . . . valuable.' Kendrick had saved himself only at the last moment from the word *crucial*.

'You mean I might identify a real rather than a would-be boyfriend?'

'Just so. I'm not implying, of course, that the art class was Mrs Hargreaves' only activity outside her home, and my team will be taking the route she took regularly to her London publishers. But the visit of the two art students to the hotel where Mrs Hargreaves was staying indicates the necessity of a very thorough investigation in that direction. Besides, at the moment it's our only lead,' Kendrick decided to add, and with a smile. Peter and Miss Bowden both returned it gratefully. 'No fingerprints on the paper, it was probably cut from a much larger piece which was touched only by gloves and a printer. Are there any computers available at the leisure complex, Miss Pym?'

'Yes. There are classes in computing, and when there isn't a class on students can go into the computer room and use the machines. And the printers. It's in the brochure. Someone'—it had been Jack Pusey—'told me that there's someone on duty for security, but he or she would hardly be interested in what students do on the computers, or what they print out.'

'No. I've decided to withhold the discovery of the note from the media, for the moment at least. So I must rely on your discretion. Do I have it?' Peter and Phyllida nodded. 'Thank you. Now, as I said, Mrs Hargreaves had a life outside the art class. For instance, I continue to be interested in her.daughter. Early on in her interview she said something to me I found a little strange. She asked me if it was possible her mother could have taken her own life, and seemed to—well, to cringe away from my answer. When I said there was no possibility at all she appeared to relax. It struck me as odd that she should have been relieved to learn her mother had been murdered. And that she should think suicide might be on the cards. It made me wonder if she knew something about what her mother was anonymously accused of.' Kendrick turned a penetrating gaze exclusively on to Phyllida.

'About which Miss Pym might encourage frankness,' Phyllida supplied obediently.

'Thank you. Is there a chance of your getting to see Sally Hargreaves?'

'I think so. I went into the library this morning, and had a piece of luck. Miss Pym fainted there yesterday, and the young man who helped Sally pick her up off the floor was working in her place, remembered the old lady, and slipped her Sally's address. So Miss Pym will be able to tell her truthfully how she got hold of it. There was a media scrum at the counter and no doubt there'll be one at the flats, but I think Miss Pym's got enough going for her to get past it. Do you know if the flats where Sally's living have entryphones, Chief Superintendent?'

'They do. Which should make things easier for you, she'll answer a buzzer where at the moment she wouldn't answer a door bell.' Miss Pym appeared to be returning his gaze, but Kendrick couldn't get rid of the absurd feeling that her eyes were disguised too and he couldn't really be looking into them. If he registered their colour he might get a chance to compare them with Mrs Sunbury's, but they were narrow and deep-set and he couldn't be sure they really were an unusual shade of violet-blue . . . It was ridiculous, Kendrick told himself, with a twitch of his heavy shoulders, to take Piper literally and screw himself up trying to believe that the woman sitting so meagre and mouselike the other side of his desk was Mrs Sunbury.

'Miss Pym's an educated woman,' Phyllida was saying. 'But she's unworldly and a bit naive, she'll be able to ask Sally questions without offence. And she won't know about the note.'

'Neither will Miss Hargreaves,' Kendrick said. 'I want to break the news to her and her father together, and I intend asking him to bring her here tomorrow morning. So this afternoon she won't be hiding, or giving away, any knowledge that has come to her via the police. If you can contrive a second visit, Miss Pym, I shall be interested to learn if knowing about the note appears to have affected her reaction to her mother's death. So far as this afternoon's visit is concerned, you might bear in mind what Jeremy Clark said in his interview about the last time he saw Mrs Hargreaves and Mrs Trenchard. He told us he was late home the night the women went to dinner at his flat, and that when he arrived Sally and her mother and Mrs Trenchard were having drinks and seemed cheerful and animated—rather hectically so, he decided, when I asked him to think very carefully. The visitors were going on about enjoying being on holiday and were full of enthusiasm about what they were going to do the next day. Perhaps that was why Mrs Trenchard had a bit of a turn after the meal and had to lie down. Clark says she seemed fine again when they said goodnight and went back to the hotel. Unfortunately they don't appear to have given any clue to any member of their families as to what they'd planned to do on the Wednesday, beyond saying it involved a drive into the country.'

'So you've no idea whether they were meeting someone—some People—by arrangement, or whether the encounter with Mrs Hargreaves' killer was a surprise to them.'

'None.'

'That picnic hamper,' Peter said musingly. 'They were on holiday and might have been expected to enjoy a few luxuries. It was cold last week, yet they chose to have a country picnic. Couldn't that indicate an assignation?'

'Possibly.'

'I wouldn't have thought,' Phyllida said, 'that the men I identified at the art class were the type of men Sally's mother would have agreed to meet.'

'Unless they were the blackmailers and she had no choice.' Peter felt himself going comfortably into the routine of his regular dialogues with Phyllida via which they sometimes reached a solution to a current problem. Then realised with a jolt where they were, and in whose company. 'I'm sorry, Chief Superintendent,' he said politely to Kendrick. 'Miss Bowden and I tend—'

'No need to apologize.' It could be that Piper might have a point in wondering if the chilly picnic had been significant.

'Thank you.' Peter hesitated. 'Could I ask you,' he went on warily. 'Why d'you think the murderer put the women on the roundabout? It was a bit elaborate.'

'Yes,' To his surprise, Kendrick found himself welcoming the opportunity to think aloud. 'I should say that if he didn't do it as a perverted joke he did it to cut out all possibility of tracing him beyond that wretched circle. And perhaps to delay the discovery of the bodies long enough to make it difficult to pinpoint the time of their deaths. As you know from the media, there was no attempt to obliterate the women's identities, so the murderer was only looking for a short-term respite. Which he got, and which has so far been enough for him. The only fibres etcetera we found on the ground or in the trees matched up with either the women or the council gardeners. And there's been no response to the plea we put out to nocturnal motorists who might have seen anything suspicious.' Kendrick wondered fleetingly if he was a closet masochist.

'Footprints?' Phyllida ventured.

'The only good thing I could think of about a roundabout as a murder scene is that no unauthorized footprint can be innocent. The trouble is, Miss Pym, that whoever deposited the bodies used his spade or some other tool to obliterate his traces as he retreated, and entered and departed via the paved route used by the gardeners.'

'But he overlooked the piece of paper in the pocket,' Peter encouraged, and was rewarded with a pained smile.

'Yes. And we'll find him,' Kendrick said, with a confidence he was far from feeling, getting to his feet and noting approvingly that Piper and Miss Pym got promptly to theirs. 'Thank you for your successful co-operation.' It didn't hurt too much.

He went with them to the door and handed them over to a constable. Then returned to his desk and rang for his DS.

'Old English Lavender Water,' Fred Wetherhead said as he crossed the room, wrinkling his nose in approval. 'My grandmother always—'

'Piper's thorough,' Kendrick interrupted shortly. The scent Anita Sunbury had left behind her had been very different.

Chapter Eight

'I'm at a loss for words. Absolutely at a loss!' Mrs Elliot's loosely sleeved arms shot upwards instead of forwards in their usual expansive gesture, as if to indicate that only the heavens could restore her power of speech. And it appeared that her plea had not been in vain: as Detective Sergeant Chaplin and Detective Constable Parsons—known jokily among their CID colleagues as the Revs since they had been teamed together—murmured their sympathy for her affliction she gainsaid it in a stream of anxious talk.

'Mrs Hargreaves and Mrs Trenchard! Such lovely ladies! Talented with watercolour, too, both of them, although that's hardly the point any longer, is it? Oh, *dear*!' When the detectives had entered the grammar school classroom Mrs Elliot had been punishing the blackboard, and as she now transferred the piece of chalk from her long fingers to the groove in front of it in another outsize gesture, DC Parsons noticed the thin drift of white powder turning in the shaft of sunlight that drilled through the large bare window. 'I heard on the radio this morning while I was making my breakfast that a woman with Seaminster connections had been murdered, and I was very shocked by that, of course, I mean, murder's a terrible thing . . . But then when I heard the name, and that Mrs Trenchard had died too, I had to sit down. I found the college stunned when I got here, absolutely stunned. I—'

'Mrs Elliot.' She had talked long enough to show DS Chaplin that, undirected, she wasn't going to be of any help. 'Look, could we go somewhere private for a few moments? I'm sure your students will manage for a little while on their own,' he went on unconfidently, looking over the fidgeting rows of rapt teenage faces, each straining to hear his soft replies to their teacher's lamentations, and imagining the fortissimo babble which would immediately follow her departure from the classroom. DC Parsons whistled under her breath.

Mrs Elliot's reflex of pleasure in the Detective Sergeant's suggestion faded a little as she too surveyed her class, but she turned back to him with a vigorous nod. 'I'll take you to the student rest room, it's unlikely there'll be anyone there so early in the day. It's in the afternoon that people wilt.' Mrs Elliot swept to the door, throwing an arm out behind her in another expansive gesture. The uproar began before they had turned the first corner, and she checked for a moment before tossing her head and flowing forward with renewed determination.

'Here we are!' Mrs Elliot threw open a door to reveal a small room which reminded both the DS and the DC of the student bedrooms they occupied in university vacations when they were on police courses. There were two chairs as well as the narrow bed, and with a gesture he was amused to find himself criticising as small and inexpressive the DS motioned Mrs Elliot to the upholstered one and Liz Parsons to the other before sitting lower than he had expected on the edge of a worn-out mattress.

Mrs Elliot sank into the armchair on a gtisty exhalation of breath. 'I still can't take it in. I mean, so young, both of them, so full of life. Although, of course, Mrs Trenchard's heart—'

'I know,' DC Parsons responded, sympathy in her soft voice and thin pale face. DS Chaplin watched her with the sibling-like affection she reciprocated and which made their working association so comfortable. 'You must have got to know them well over the months ... years ... How long had they been coming to your class, Mrs Elliot?'

'From the beginning!' Mrs Elliot announced, in a sort of triumph. 'From the very first!'

'Which was?'

'Five years ago,' she told them, after a pause to count in silence on her spectacularly ringed fingers. 'It has to be, because I started teaching here the autumn of the year my husband passed away.'

The detectives turned on an instant to look briefly at one another, both surprised that the widow had spoken of so basic a loss without pause or emotion, both wondering if it was because she felt none, or because five years had been long enough for her to work through those particular histrionics. 'The leisure complex was all leisure up till then, which seemed to me a great waste of resources, and when I'd persuaded the local authority to give me an adult class they agreed to allow other classes on other nights of the week. I have no difficulty maintaining order, but with adult people who *choose* to learn, order is not an issue and teaching them is particularly pleasant.'

'I can imagine,' the DS lied, while DC Parsons nodded understandingly. 'And I can also imagine that once people join your class they tend to stay.' He paused, to give Mrs Elliot time to preen at his compliment, wondering on a shiver of surprise if his transfer to the CID was turning him into the polished cat he had always jeered at his colleagues for showing signs of becoming. And Liz Parsons was smiling down at her knees. 'So I suppose they become very much at home with one another, friendly . . .'

'Sergeant!' Mrs Elliot's voice was shocked, but her eyes were excited. 'What are you saying? Are you suggesting that Mrs Hargreaves met her killer *here*? In my class?' In a high-kicking gesture of her long black shoes, she reversed the order of her crossed knees.

'I'm not suggesting anything, Mrs Elliot. I'm merely seeking information on one aspect of her life. My colleagues at this very moment will be questioning other people with whom she—and Mrs Trenchard—came into contact.'

'Yes. Of course.' Chaplin thought he saw a flash of disappointment. 'And you're quite right, you know.' Mrs Elliot rallied, leaning forwards. 'My students *do* feel at home with one another, they *are* friendly. One friendship a couple of years ago even ended in *marriage*'

'You must have been pleased about that,' DC Parsons observed.

'I was! They were terribly sweet, invited me to the wedding, said I was their good angel . . .'

DS Chaplin heard himself say 'How very nice,' and decided yes, he was changing, at least on the job. He hadn't noticed himself becoming different off duty but he'd have to watch it. 'What about the other side of the coin, though? Have you been aware at all lately of any bad feeling among your students? Anything involving Mrs Hargreaves and perhaps Mrs Trenchard?' He knew the words of the note by heart and kept repeating them in his head.

'No!' But Mrs Elliot wasn't looking quite so positive as she had sounded. 'Not what I would call *bad feeling*,' she went on, speaking more slowly than her usual headlong pace.

'Just the opposite, I suppose you could say . . . I try not to notice all the nuances,' she said, Chaplin thought sensibly. And I don't think it's a good thing for the teacher to get too involved in student fun. But some things one can't help noticing, of course, and . . .'

'Yes?' the DC prompted, pen poised and hiding her eagerness, to Chaplin's approval.

'There's been a sort of an ongoing joke,' Mrs Elliot told them reluctantly. 'Ever since the two ladies joined, really. Two men I—well, I was a bit surprised when they enrolled, to be honest, they didn't look the sort, but then I discovered that one of them—Gary Jones—has the makings of a really exciting watercolourist and had been persuaded to come by a third member of the class, Jack Rubin, who has an eye for an artist. I hope Gary's friend, Desmond Wilkins, is enjoying himself here, too,' Mrs Elliot added tactfully.

'So what have you to tell us about these two men, Mrs Elliot?' DC Chaplin was discovering that he had stopped seeing Mrs Elliot as a big laugh and was beginning to respect her. He was glad to see that Liz appeared to be taking her statement down verbatim. 'The joke . . .'

'Mrs Trenchard and Mrs Hargreaves were both attractive in their different ways,' Mrs Elliot said apologetically, and Liz Parsons wondered if she saw herself as responsible for her adult students' moral welfare as well as their artistic development. And the men, well, they weren't the type to be backward in coming forward. They made it obvious from the beginning that they admired the ladies—Mr Wilkins Mrs Hargreaves and Mr Jones Mrs

Trenchard—and the class, well, the class backed them up in a jokey sort of way, like a chorus in a Greek play, you could say.'

'I see.' DC Chaplin thought he did, without ever having read, or seen, a Greek play. He wondered fleetingly if Liz shared his ignorance.

'It would be hard to believe the men were really expecting the ladies to respond,' Mrs Elliot went swiftly on. 'The whole thing was ... well, *public*, you might say. And because they obviously didn't feel threatened, the ladies didn't raise any objections, they just smiled and turned every personal remark the men made aside. It must have been like trying to climb a slippery slope. If the men really were trying, that is, and as I said, I doubt if either of them was ever alone with his *inamorata*, and I don't think there was anyone in the class who took them seriously, certainly not to the extent where they would ...' At last Mrs Elliot faltered. Liz Parsons looked up from her flying ballpoint and saw that the wide brown eyes (she didn't think she had ever seen eyes with such large, clear whites), were, for the first time, troubled. 'Oh, dear,' Mrs Elliot went on. 'I wish now I hadn't said anything, it was so, well, so *superficial*. And the ladies never put the men down at all, they didn't do anything to hurt their egos. Male egos, you know ...' This time Mrs Elliot clapped a hand over her mouth. 'I'm sorry, Sergeant,' she said, in a subdued voice he was already able to register as uncharacteristic.

'That's all right, Madam.' DS Chaplin tried not to notice that Liz was smiling again as she wrote. And it was more important to record some unexpectedly insightful remarks than to spare his feelings. Anyway, the idea that the male ego was more touchy than the female wasn't a new one to him, his current girlfriend had put it to him a number of times. 'Don't worry about having told us about the two men,' he went on. 'From what you've said about the set-up I expect everyone else in the class will tell us, too.'

DS Chaplin smiled at Mrs Elliot as he watched the tension release her face, and DC Parsons said softly, 'So you won't mind telling us the men's names again so that we can confirm—'

'Des Wilkins and Gary Jones. I never thought there was any

harm in them. Especially Gary Jones. If there had been—any mischief—Mr Wilkins would have been the leader.'

'There probably isn't any harm in either of them,' Chaplin said. 'But you'll appreciate we have to look into every contact the ladies have recently had. Especially as finding the bodies on a traffic island makes it pretty impossible to work from that end of things.'

The extraordinary eyes were now enormous. 'Yes. It must do. I hadn't thought . . . I just thought, what a terrible risk.'

'One the murderer must have considered worth taking. If it came off, the bodies might as well be in a sterile bubble.'

'Not quite, Sergeant, surely? There has to have been contact—'

'Well, as good as.' The over-the-top comparison had been made by the Chief, and Chaplin had felt the frustration like an aura around the tall angry man with the wild curls, to the extent that he had looked down at his knees so as not to meet the sparking eyes. 'Now, Mrs Elliot, did the ladies drive themselves to the class, and did they come together?'

'So far as I know they always came in their own car. And together.'

'Thank you. Do you have a party at Christmas?'

'Yes.' Mrs Elliot didn't look surprised. She didn't know about the piece of paper, but she knew what he was getting at. 'We have great fun. But even then Mrs Hargreaves and Mrs Trenchard, they never got carried away, never behaved any differently, even after a couple of glasses of wine. One or two of us have gone home a little cheerful, but I've never seen anyone overstep the mark. Or as if they might if they got the opportunity. And that includes the two lads, Mr Chaplin.'

'I see. Now, Mrs Elliot, is there anything else at all you can tell us about Mrs Hargreaves and Mrs Trenchard's relations with other students?'

'The ladies hadn't really made any friends in the class,' Mrs Elliot responded obliquely, after a pause in which she fiddled with a ring. 'I suppose because they had each other's company. Oh, they were friendly enough, with everyone, but only to the extent of a few words at coffee time and some generous remarks . . . Oh!'

'You've thought of something,' DC Parsons coaxed.

'Well, yes, but not ... Young Paul Denton is unemployed, and got quite enthusiastic when Mrs Hargreaves told him about her book-jacket work, thinking he might try something similar. I overheard them one break, where Mrs Hargreaves gave him a name and address—I think it was of her agent. She said she'd be happy to look at any work he thought might be suitable ... Oh, dear ...' For a moment Mrs Elliot's prevailing expression had been reminiscently happy, but now a cloud came over it as transforming as a cloud across the sun. 'There was nothing remotely *sinister* about it, it was just one person trying to help another, I was glad to see it, to feel that my class might have been the means to set young Paul on a career. Mrs Hargreaves and Mrs Trenchard, they really are—were—*nice people*' Mrs Elliot sank back in her chair. 'I've just realized ... I've just *really realized* ...'

'It's all right,' DC Parsons said gently, as they saw the tears. They sat in silence until Mrs Elliot had blown her nose, then got slowly to their feet, thinking for the umpteenth time in unison. 'Thank you for being so patient and cooperative,' Chaplin said. 'DC Parsons will write up what you've told us and someone will come back to you to ask you to sign it.'

Mrs Elliot looked startled. 'I've made a statement, have I?'

'Yes,' Liz Parsons said. And a very helpful one. Thank you, Mrs Elliot. The only other thing we have to ask you for is a list of the names and addresses of all the members of your class.' She glanced at Chaplin as Chaplin glanced at her, and each knew the other's fervent hope that the class was small.

'Of course. I'll get it from the office if you don't mind waiting a minute, they've got a photocopier.'

'Is it a large class?' Liz ventured, as Mrs Elliot drifted past her.

'Sixteen people,' the teacher responded proudly. Then said, 'I mean fourteen,' in a muffled voice as she pulled the door to.

The detectives exchanged grimaces.

'Not too bad, Jack,' Liz observed. 'I'd've expected more, I'm sure she's an inspiring teacher. And I've decided I like her.'

'Me too. Although at first ...'

'Yes. Have we learned anything? Apart from Mrs Elliot's admirable outlook on life?'

Jack Chaplin shrugged. 'Confirmation's always worth having. And I'd say we've learned all that *she* knows.'

But when Mrs Elliot returned with the photocopies she told them she had not been entirely frank.

'Yes, Mrs Elliot?' Liz Parsons invited, her notebook back in her hand.

'I'm sorry I said there wasn't anything else,' she told them. 'There is. At least—well, I've decided you should know although I hate telling tales.'

'This is murder,' the detectives said sternly and in unison, just managing to suppress their amusement.

'I know, that's why . . . well. There's a student—a woman'—not a lady, both interrogators noted—'quite young I should say, but she acts and dresses rather middle-aged. When she first joined the class she made overtures, but I'm afraid there was—is—something about her that makes people disinclined to respond. She doesn't have inspiration as a painter, either, so I've tended to feel sorry for her. But I discovered recently that she was jealous of Mrs Trenchard and Mrs Hargreaves, because even though they are—were—reserved they had *charisma*, you know? And, well, the men liked it, liked them. I was in a cubicle in the ladies' room not long ago during the break'—Liz Parsons had to suppress a smile again as Mrs Elliot blushed—'and I heard this woman talking to another woman who's not unlike her but who doesn't, well, doesn't *try* as hard as Miss Cummings tries, so that everyone's quite easy with her.'

'This is very helpful,' Liz prompted, as Mrs Elliot paused.

'I heard Miss Cummings say something like' "I hate women like those two." Then the other said "Which two?" and Miss Cummings said their names. Then she said she knew their type, they led men on then backed off. She said there were times it made her feel sick, to see all the men around them. "What they want is a good hiding," she said, and the other woman protested and then they both went out. Oh, dear . . .' Mrs Elliot looked at the detectives imploringly.

'Have I done right to tell you? We all say things we don't really mean, and I don't want to get anyone into trouble.'

'Of course you've done right,' Liz Parsons said gently, 'and you'll probably be backed up by your students again. What you've just told us will go into your statement. Now, is there anything else?'

'No! I promise you!'

'Thank you.' Both Chaplin and Parsons believed her, and got to their feet.

'The young man with the book jackets,' DC Parsons asked, ballpoint poised.

'Paul Denton,' Mrs Elliot supplied reluctantly. 'And Miss Elizabeth Cummings.'

'So, not all negative,' Liz said as they fastened their seat belts. 'But if you were blackmailing someone, wouldn't you keep a low public profile?'

'Unless you thought you were clever enough to work a double bluff. Or pretend you were in contact for a different reason. Which couldn't apply to the woman.'

All the same, the men could be red herrings. Perhaps the dead women really were just flirts.'

'Perhaps. And we've still got to canvas each and every member of the class,'

Both detectives groaned, but then grinned. They were, in fact, enjoying themselves enormously.

When, in mid-afternoon, Miss Pym approached the small three-storey block in which Jeremy Clark owned a flat, there were a mere three pressmen hanging about outside, none of whom came noticeably to attention as they saw her. She spread her gloved hand over several in the vertical row of bells as she pressed number six, and the pressmen continued to look bored and frustrated. The advantages of being Miss Pym were becoming steadily more obvious to her creator. When a wary female voice asked who it was, Phyllida matched her voice even more precisely than she had matched it in the library to Miss Pym's insignificant appearance.

'It's Agnes Pym, dear,' she said apologetically. 'From the library.

Stephen was reluctant, but in the end he let me have your address.' The pressmen might be lolling against the wall as negligently as Steve lolled against office doorposts, but they had to be listening.

Phyllida felt herself tensing into the pause, but it ended with Sally saying, 'Come in, Miss Pym. Top floor. Please don't let anyone else into the building.'

'Of course not, dear.' But the electronically channelled voice had carried, and Miss Pym only just managed to slip through the briefly buzzing door before the men were upon it.

After a plunge up the first half dozen stairs in one of those flashes of forgetfulness Phyllida had reluctantly accepted that no amount of professional planning and experience could entirely eliminate, she slowed to an old lady pace, and Sally was standing warily at her open front door as, breathing heavily, she rounded the last of the six short flights. Sally's blotched face—grief seemed to have made it slightly lopsided—lit up for a moment as she saw Miss Pym, and she held out a hand.

'Come in, come in! How very kind of you. But I knew you were nice when we met in the library.'

'Not at all, Sally, I was concerned for you.' And for herself, as for an unnerving instant Phyllida too saw Miss Pym as a real person and also approved her sweet nature. Are you alone?'

'Yes, but it's all right. Daddy was here for lunch and Jeremy'll be home early . . .' Sally's voice had lost its sparkle and the dilation of her pupils made her eyes look dark. 'The doctor gave me something,' she said, as after a wary look towards the stairs she closed the door. 'It's made me feel a bit far away and not quite in charge. So once I start talking I talk too much. And I forget things like asking you to sit down. I'm sorry, please come into the sitting-room.'

Jeremy Clark's sitting-room was a rectangle, one of its long sides all window with a panoramic view of the sea over a descent of old roofs. Before turning reluctantly away, Phyllida saw that the clouds which had obscured the colours of the early morning were knifed low down on the horizon by a thin gold line.

'What a lovely view!' Miss Pym observed as she sat down on the edge of the armchair Sally indicated.

'Yes. I loved it.'

Phyllida found the past tense acutely sad. 'Put the kettle on, dear,' Miss Pym advised. 'I'd love a cup and I expect you could do with one, too.'

The girl's face brightened at the prospect, Phyllida thought, of filling a few nightmare moments with a comfortably distracting task. 'Yes! You'll have a biscuit too, won't you?'

'Thank you, dear.'

Sally was away a little longer than it could have taken to make tea, but when she came back with a tray in her hands she managed a brief smile.

'I'd have gone back home,' she said as she set it down on the low table between the armchairs in the window. 'But Daddy's staying with Frank because Frank's just about collapsed ... I don't have to explain who Frank is, do I?' she said, with a sudden ferocity that made Phyllida jump. 'Or my father? You read the papers and you listen to the news.'

'Yes, dear. Oh, I'm so very, very sorry.'

'I know you are, Miss Pym,' Sally said, reverting to her new soft monotone. 'And I'm really grateful. Especially that you actually came to see me.' For the first time Sally looked at Phyllida rather than through her. Are *you* all right? I should have asked you ages ago.'

'I'm fine, Sally. Really.'

'I'm glad. Milk and sugar?'

'A very little milk. No sugar.' Eating and drinking were two of the few areas into which Phyllida did not force herself to extend her professionalism.

'There you go.' Sally put the cup and saucer on the small table beside Miss Pym's chair and offered a plate of assorted biscuits.

'Tell me,' Miss Pym asked, as she took one, 'have the police any clues as to who committed this terrible crime? Oh, dear ...' she went on as she registered Sally's jerk of discomfort and the way her eyes slid aside. 'Forgive me, Sally, of course you couldn't tell me even if there was anything to tell. I didn't think, I just wanted—'

'That's all right, Miss Pym. No, they don't seem to have anything to tell us at the moment.' Having recovered from her shock, Sally was now looking Phyllida frankly in the eyes.

So she could lie convincingly. 'I'm sorry, dear. We mustn't talk of it,' Phyllida said reluctantly.

'I don't mind. Not with you. And I can't think about anything else so I might as well talk about it. It helps, actually, in a way.' Sally's eyes flashed, and her voice was suddenly fierce again. 'One of the tabloid papers suggested this morning that Mummy and Maggie could have been meeting men. That was wicked, they weren't. I *know* they weren't.'

'Because you know *them*, of course.'

It was an innocent enough remark, even a kindly one, and Phyllida jerked again at the girl's violent reaction.

'What d'you mean?' Sally demanded, her face flaming and her eyes wide and angry. 'What do you mean by that?'

Miss Pym shrank back in her chair. 'Sally, please! I only meant that you know your mother and her friend aren't the kind of women who would betray their marriages. I was just agreeing with you that how you read them is how they are.'

'How they are ... yes, of course.' The anger in Sally's eyes had given way to bewilderment. She got up and came to kneel in front of Miss Pym's chair, taking her hand. 'Miss Pym, I'm so sorry. I'm just ... ultrasensitive since I read the piece in that horrible rag. I'm sorry I jumped on you, but I *know* they weren't meeting any men. The idea's disgusting.'

'I'm very much afraid some other aspect of the media may suggest it too,' Miss Pym said. 'Trial by media is the phrase nowadays, isn't it? The poor Prime Minister, for example ... It's not a nice thing.'

'The worst part of it is that you can't answer back, can't tell them how obscenely wrong they are.'

'Only, I suppose, if you have something positive to show them they're wrong. Your mother and her friend hadn't told you anything about what they were going to-do when they went into the country that day?'

'No. Nothing.' But to Phyllida's surprise Sally's eyes slid away from hers again, and her face flamed.

'It was some madman, of course,' Miss Pym reassured her. 'But I suppose that doesn't sound as interesting to certain sections of the media as—well, as something personal. And I suppose high-powered journalists sometimes forget that the people they're writing about are real and can suffer. You mustn't let them destroy you, Sally.'

Sally squeezed the old lady's hand before getting to her feet and going back to her chair. 'You're a dear, and you're absolutely right' Her face, now, wore its usual innocent, uncomplicated expression, but suffused with a sorrow which might affect the look of it for the rest of her life.

'May I come again?' Phyllida asked, as much out of her pang of sympathy as the promptings of her job.

'Oh, please do! And I'll hope to see you in the library in a couple of weeks—I've been told to take a week or two off and then see how I feel. If it wasn't for the media I'd go back tomorrow but at the moment I couldn't take that.'

'I should think not! Anyway, they're very fickle, you know, dear, they'll get tired of you.'

'Unless the police find the murderer.'

'They will, Sally!' Miss Pym urged eagerly. 'The police are really very clever.' Particularly when assisted by the Peter Piper Detective Agency. 'You'll see.' Miss Pym looked round the room. 'This is a very nice flat. I'm afraid I know from the media, too, that it belongs to your friend, Jeremy. I'm sure he must be a great comfort.'

'Oh, he is!' The same uncomplicatedly joyous reaction Phyllida had seen when Sally had told Miss Pym she had recently come to live in Seaminster. And he gets on so well with Mummy and Daddy. *Shit*!' Sally shouted, leaping to her feet. 'How can L still say something like that? I'll never be able to accept Mummy's dead. Never, never, never!'

'You will,' Miss Pym said softly. 'But what you must never do is stop talking about her.' As Phyllida, at her father's urging, had once talked about her own dead mother. 'To your father, to Jeremy, to everyone who knew her.'

'She was lovely,' Sally said, on a dreadful sob. 'Well, you know she was lovely to look at, you've seen the photographs. Not pretty in the sort of very feminine way Maggie was . . .' Sally stopped, staring at Miss Pym in a return of the bewilderment Phyllida wondered if she was imagining, while knowing she wasn't.

'They looked very different,' Miss Pym agreed. 'But both so nice-looking in their own ways.'

'You're so kind,' Sally said. 'I'm sorry I swore at you.'

'You didn't.' Phyllida saw a tic at work beside one red-rimmed eye, and got to her feet. There were further questions for Miss Pym to ask, but they would be more fruitfully answered on her second visit. 'You've had enough, Sally. Try to rest now until Jeremy comes home. And I expect you'll be cooking a meal.'

'Yes.' Again the instant of pathetic brightness, at the prospect of another diversion. 'Ring me, if you'd like to,' Sally said, as she led the way to the door. 'Here . . .' She stopped in the hall by a small table on which were a pad and pen, scribbled some figures and handed Miss Pym the torn off square. 'Then we can fix a time for you to come again. Or I can ring you?'

Phyllida was ready. 'Better, I think, for me to ring you, dear. I live with a cousin, and she prefers it if I don't have calls.' Miss Pym had managed not to sound either deprived or pathetic, but Phyllida saw with satisfaction Sally's brief forgetting of her own ills in her realization that her new friend was a poor relation. 'So I'll ring you,' she promised cheerfully.

'Thank you, Miss Pym, I hope you will. It's a funny thing,' Sally said, looking slightly surprised, 'But I'm discovering that when—at a time like this—someone you don't know is easier to talk to than someone you do. Not that I mean that I don't know you, Miss Pym.'

'I understand what you mean, dear. Goodbye.'

'Goodbye, and thank you so much for coming.' To Phyllida's pleasure and dismay, Sally flung her arms round Miss Pym, for a moment endangering her hat and hair. A reminder, Phyllida reflected ruefully as Miss Pym went carefully down the stairs, of how essential it was for her characters to limit social contact. Which no doubt would feel less of a penance if she herself had the will and the energy to recreate a personal life.

Chapter Nine

When Gary Jones first wakened he was nothing but a warm, comfortable body stretching relaxed limbs, aware merely of the light patterning the ceiling and the sound of voices and traffic beyond his bedroom window. It was only as he realized in grateful surprise that, despite the drinking he had done the night before, his head was clear that he also realised why he had felt the need for so many beers and chasers. Then he turned towards his bedside clock with a groan as the panic flooded back, frantic with regret. If only he'd stood up to Des, refused to go along with his crazy ideas . . .

Almost eight o'clock. Not too early, in their nightmare circumstances, to ring Des and try to ease the panic by talking it out. After he'd heard the latest news . . . Gary knocked the clock to the floor as he stretched out an arm, but he carried on fumbling for the knob of the radio and eventually turned it on.

A train crash in Chile was a respite, postponing the tightening movement the panic was poised to make. And which, when it came, persuaded him for a few ghastly seconds that he was choking.

> *. . . The police say they have a lead in their investigation into the murder of one of two women whose bodies were recently discovered on a traffic island outside the coastal town of Seaminster . . .*

He made it to the bathroom just in time to throw up into the lavatory basin. While he was still there, crouched on the floor and gasping, he heard the telephone and staggered back to the bedroom, where he burrowed down in the bed before grabbing the receiver.

'Yes! Hello!'

'Des here.' The usual low monotone, but Gary had already discovered that however churned up Des might be there were never any outward signs of it. 'Hear the news?'

'Yes. Des . . .'

'Try to stop wheezing. You'll have guilt written all over you.'

'A lead . . . D'you think the police . . .?'

'Of course. The gay barman is sure to identify us.'

'Christ, yes. Des . . .' Gary tried desperately to inject confidence into the feeble voice he was listening to like it was someone else's. 'We made a mistake, didn't we, going to the hotel?'

'We didn't think things would turn out like they did.'

'God, no. Anyway, the class thing was so jokey, probably no one—'

'Almost certainly someone. Ma Elliot for a start, she sees more than she lets on.'

'Oh, God, Des . . .'

'Look.' Des Wilkins sat up to light a cigarette and approve his bare upper torso in the mirrored cupboard door at the foot of his bed, lamenting on a reflex that it was unaccompanied by one with boobs. 'We've got to be ready for the worst scenario, accept that once the police find out about the class and the hotel—which they will—they'll pick us up. Which means we've got to get together before they arrive to agree how we're going to play it. What sort of a day have you got? Is it heavy?'

'It doesn't have to be. You?'

'Me neither. Best to postpone our respective offs and meet now. I'll come over.'

Which made it convenient for the police when, having drawn a blank at Des Wilkins's flat on the eastern outskirts of Seaminster, they went on to Gary Jones's to the west of the town and found the two sales reps together.

Before ringing Peter Piper to say he'd be obliged if he could spare him another visit, Kendrick promised himself he'd hide his satisfaction that it was his own staff rather than the staff of the Peter Piper Agency who had made the latest art class discoveries. Even though the immediate outcome of their success was the necessity of asking the Agency to extend its brief, Kendrick's ever-ready irritation remained at bay. But that, he reflected through the unfamiliar warmth which for the past twenty-four hours had suffused a mind and a body so long grown cold, had to be the result of his estranged but still beloved wife Miriam agreeing for the first time to remain when she brought their daughter over next Sunday for his statutory time with her.

Dr Piper agreed to come at eleven that morning, with the instant polite compliance which told Kendrick nothing of his real reactions.

'I'd like to see Miss Bowden, too.' Despite his miraculous new sense of personal hope, Kendrick's request was still reluctant.

'Certainly, Chief Superintendent.'

Peter finished his coffee and came out of his room to find Phyllida, Steve and Jenny drinking theirs together in Reception, Jenny at her desk, Phyllida in a client's chair and Steve supported by a doorpost. Aware of Phyllida's desire to keep abreast of the youngsters' states of mind and morale and approving it, Peter beamed on them before telling Phyllida apologetically that the Chief Superintendent wanted to see him and Miss Bowden again within the hour.

'He needs Mrs Sunbury to work on those travelling salesmen!' In his excitement Steve detached himself from the doorpost and took his own weight.

'An interesting thesis,' Peter said. 'But I don't believe it. Thanks to Phyllida his own officers should be at work on them by now.'

'If they're innocent,' Jenny said worriedly, 'it'll be a nightmare for them.'

'So far as we know they're the only lead,' Peter reminded her. 'So the police have to start with them. It could turn out to be unfair, or it could solve the murder.' He turned to Phyllida. 'Fiona Steele, do you think? With the art class being the centre of attention at the moment she seems appropriate and I think the Chief Superintendent should be given a look at her.'

Phyllida agreed. 'And her bits and pieces are at the Golden Lion.'

'You shouldn't talk about her like that!' Steve looked shocked, and Jenny told him not to be silly.

'The Chief Super should find her a nice change from Miss Pym,' Peter said.

The Chief Super, to his unwelcome surprise, found Mrs Steele attractive. In a different way from Mrs Sunbury, although they shared the same wide and indubitably violet-coloured eyes. But he couldn't accept that they were the same woman, and as for Miss Pym . . .

'Yesterday a couple of my officers went to the computer room at the leisure complex,' he said without preamble as he lifted the coffee pot, hoping the serious business of murder would push his continuing bewilderment into the background. They typed the message found on Mrs Hargreaves' body on each of the machines there, and printed it out on each of the printers. I've learned this morning that one of their efforts matches the note. Yesterday, as well, two CID officers interviewed Mrs Elliot, and discovered two other possible connections with Mrs Hargreaves among her students.' Kendrick told himself it was childish to feel one up. 'A young man by the name of Paul Denton, unemployed, discovered that Mrs Hargreaves designed book jackets, and was fired with the idea of doing this himself. Apparently Mrs Hargreaves encouraged him, to the extent of giving him her agent's name and address. She also said she'd be happy to look at anything he tried to do in that line. Did you notice him?' he asked Phyllida.

'I think so. There was only one really young man.'

The usual voice, and for a surreal moment Kendrick: wondered if Dr Piper was a ventriloquist with a series of dummies. 'Then there's Miss Elizabeth Cummings,' he went on quickly. 'A maiden lady of indeterminate age who was overheard by Mrs Elliot in the ladies' cloakroom expressing her disgust at the way the two victims attracted men, and her opinion that they deserved a good hiding. Those, Mrs Elliot was certain, were the words she used. Were you aware of *her*?'

'Yes.'

'I'd like you to observe her,' Kendrick said. 'And Denton. And the other members of the class, with the exception of two young girls who were in Greece when Mrs Hargreaves was murdered. Will you do that?'

'Of course.'

Phyllida and Kendrick both looked at Peter, who nodded.

'I've already spoken to Miss Cummings,' Phyllida told the Chief Superintendent. Kendrick found he had been expecting her to say that, but he seemed to be getting used to her pre-empting him. 'Well, she spoke to me and we went out together in a break to get coffee. I knew her name because she'd signed it very large on a dreadful painting.' She paused as she brought out a memory she had perhaps accorded too little significance. 'I remember now ... When the men started talking to Fiona Miss Cummings snorted and flounced off.'

'As with the men,' Peter said, 'if she was guilty of attempted blackmail, wouldn't you expect her to have kept a low profile?'

'If she was confident Mrs Hargreaves was going to keep quiet and pay up,' Kendrick said, 'she might have thought it didn't matter. Whatever, without forensic help I have to investigate every possible lead.' His ever-ready mental picture of the roundabout in its sterile surround rose before his inward eye, but to his surprise the irritability it had so far engendered in him was routed even as it appeared by his new sense of personal hope.

'I don't think Miss Cummings is used to social success,' Phyllida said. 'Which should make her responsive to a friendly overture.' But not become a millstone round Fiona's neck for ever after, because Fiona wouldn't be there to suffer her. There were pros as well as cons to forming relationships in character.

'So see what you can do. With them all except for the two young women.' Kendrick relaxed slightly into his chair.

'And the two old men?' Phyllida suggested. 'They really are quite decrepit, they come and go in a nursing home minibus.'

'Except for the two old men, then. For the time being. What's left of the bodies is being released today, by the way. I've asked to be informed of the date of the funeral, which no doubt one of you will discover as soon as it's decided.' Kendrick paused, then fixed Dr Piper with a suddenly sharp gaze. 'Anyone who wishes to may attend a funeral, of course, and observation when people are off their guard can yield surprisingly fruitful results. Which I'm sure you have discovered, Dr Piper.'

'I have, yes.'

Kendrick turned to Phyllida. 'My first art class interviews are with the two reps. Can you embellish your report on them in any way, Mrs Steele?' To his annoyance the Chief Superintendent was aware of a dual excitement: the prospect of being offered a clue to Miss Bowden in the degree of her interaction with 'Mrs Steele' as well as the prospect of learning something in advance about his prime suspects.

Phyllida considered. 'They were so similar in type I didn't see right away how different they were in their physical appearance. It took a bit longer still—I was in the pub—for me to realise that Des Wilkins was the leader. The other man I mentioned in my report—Jack Pusey, who took us in his car to the pub—he seemed to be in the role of an indulgent uncle to the other two, stern but affectionate though I think that was just another bit of role-playing.' Phyllida paused, then went on reluctantly. 'Jack Pusey was the person who gave me the details about the women, that they were staying in Seaminster at the Fountains Hotel. Just quoting what they'd told the class, he said. I'm sorry, it didn't seem—'

'Your report was adequate, Miss Bowden. And I appreciate that, unlike the police, you can only work obliquely.'

'Thank you.'

'Now,' Kendrick went on, when he had drained his coffee cup. 'There's the implication in the note to consider. If we're looking for a blackmailer in the art class, then that has to be the most likely place to look for the person Mrs Hargreaves is accused of carrying on with. Would you say there was anyone there, Mrs Steele, who might fit that bill?'

'There's no one who seems *likely*,' Phyllida said, dismissing a. sudden sharp vision of Jack Pusey's smile. 'But there are two men of round about Mrs Hargreave's age—the class jester who everybody likes, and an unrestful man with gimlet eyes who everybody seems to dislike. Paul Denton, if I've got the right chap, is a lot younger, but would make a nice toyboy. And there's Jack Pusey, the friend of Gary and Des, he'd be around the right age, I suppose. Again, I'm leaving the old men out of it.'

'All right. But the men you've mentioned, if you can try to think of them from both points of view, adulterer and blackmailer.'

'Or one and the same?' Peter suggested. 'Someone could have had his way with Mrs Hargreaves, then decided to capitalise on it.'

'It's possible,' Kendrick agreed reluctantly. 'But from what you've already said, Mrs Steele, you don't see either Wilkins or Jones as likely boyfriends.'

'I think they're less likely than some of the other men. But I'll try to keep an open mind.'

'I'm sure you will. Now, Miss Pym saw Miss Hargreaves yesterday?'

'Yes.' Phyllida pushed a sheet of paper across the desk. 'Miss Hargreaves seemed pleased, gave her tea and said she hoped she'd come again.' Phyllida hesitated. 'Mr Kendrick . . .'

'Yes?'

'You said . . . You told us you got the impression Sally Hargreaves was relieved to learn that her mother couldn't have taken her own life.'

'Yes?'

'Well, Sally didn't tell Miss Pym anything specific about her mother, and you told us she didn't know about the note, but I got the feeling that something to do with her mother is worrying her over and above her anguish at her death. She's so—well, so *confident* she couldn't have had an assignation, it's as if she has some knowledge. And once or twice when she was talking about the murder to Miss Pym—she said she found her easy to talk to, which is lucky—she looked terrified, and then, well, *bewildered*. Oh, it's all nuances, probably I was just looking too hard for something then blowing up what was perfectly natural. I know from experience that grief can take what seems to other people like illogical forms.'

'Yes.' Kendrick pushed aside thoughts of his own situation in that light. Then read the entreaty in the eyes across his desk. 'Sally Hargreaves and her father were both here earlier and I told them about the discovery of the note. Both of them reacted with an impressive show of shocked surprise. It's been in my mind that to pre-empt the blackmailer Mrs Hargreaves could have told her husband about the behaviour of which the note accuses her, and that he could then have killed her—strangulation, if one has the strength or the fury, can be the most spontaneous of murder methods—but, if so, his insistence that his wife was true to him would make him a remarkably fine actor. The daughter seemed just as outraged. And now that we know where the note was printed . . .'

Peter thanked the Chief Superintendent for his frankness.

'I still need your help.' Kendrick got to his feet. 'The funeral,' he said. 'Sometimes nuances, when one is in a position to read them . . .'

'I know,' Peter responded. 'Miss Bowden and I—independently, of course—will go to the funeral.'

To his displeased surprise, Kendrick found himself smiling a slightly conspiratorial smile.

One piece of Miss Bowden's information Kendrick hadn't needed was the information that the dark chap was the leader; he was pale and composed where the fair one dripped sweat down his temples and had terrified question marks for eyes. If he was left to soften up any further he could collapse beyond usefulness, whereas the dark one had plenty of cool to lose.

'Get Gary Jones into an interview room,' Kendrick ordered DS Wetherhead when he had handed Dr Piper and Miss Bowden over to a uniform, 'and stay there. I want you sitting in with me.'

When Kendrick joined the two men ten minutes later Gary Jones had his head down on his arms. Kendrick didn't know how long he and Wilkins had been getting their act together when the police found them that morning, but with luck this one would have been too panicked to make the best of the time they'd had. As Kendrick sat down and motioned to his DS to start and introduce the tape, Gary Jones sat up and stared at the two policemen in what looked like the panic of an innocent man with no means of proving his innocence. But Kendrick had had his prime suspects over the years who had looked like terrified toddlers and been guilty as hell, and he didn't find it hard to reserve judgment.

'Right, son,' he said in a kindly way, and the pale blue eyes blinked in relieved surprise. 'Now, I'd like you to tell me why you and your friend Des Wilkins chose the Fountains Hotel for a drink the night before one of your art class mates—Mrs Carol Hargreaves—was murdered. But I don't want you to tell me you didn't know she was staying there, because I know that you did.'

'The whole class knew!'

'But it was only you and Des who did anything with the knowledge. Was that because Mrs Hargreaves—and perhaps her friend, Mrs Trenchard—invited you?'

'No!' Gary Jones's shocked reaction made Kendrick begin to hope he really was as naive as he looked.

'So why did you go?'

'We . . . look!' Jones leaned imploringly across the table. 'It was just the same jokey thing as in the class. We had a sort of thing going, that we were hopelessly in love with them. *Hopelessly.* Everyone, Mrs Hargreaves and Mrs Trenchard too, knew it was a joke.'

'But when you saw a chance to meet them away from the class, you thought it might become more serious?'

'*No!* We just thought—well, they were in Seaminster, in a place where we had a right to be too, and if we went to the hotel we just might see them. Persuade them to have a drink with us. That was *all!*' Gary Jones almost wailed.

'All right, son. Enjoy your class, do you? I hear you're a rather good painter.'

'So they tell me,' Gary Jones blew his nose.

'Go to any other classes in the leisure complex?'

'We went to computers last year. Des had bought himself a more sophisticated one, and thought it might help.' The same open face, wide eyes. Gary Jones was either pathetically naive, or not naive at all.

'Even if you don't go to the computer class you can still use the computers, can't you?'

'That's right,' The eyes were still meeting Kendrick's.

'Did you leave the bar at all, that night at the Fountains?'

'What?' Kendrick thought Jones had come to attention. Perhaps he had put more effort into appearing unfazed about the computers than about the drink at the Fountains. 'No! Unless you count going to the toilet.'

'Did you take this with you when you went, and push it under Mrs Hargreaves' door?' Kendrick laid the note on the table in front of Jones. 'It was found on her body. And printed out at the leisure complex.'

'No! Dear God, no!' Gary Jones looked up from the note with anguished eyes. 'I've never seen it before this moment, God's honour! And I didn't know, neither of us knew, the number of Mrs Hargreaves' room!'

'Well, there are other ways you could have delivered it,' Kendrick said, retrieving the note.

'But I didn't, Des didn't. You've got to believe me!' To Kendrick's embarrassment the appeal in his eyes was liquifying and threatening to overflow. Fred Wetherhead coughed and shuffled his feet. 'And we didn't murder them, we never even saw them on their own. In the class or out of it. Des'll tell you.'

'The way you've told us? The way you agreed between you?' Wetherhead suggested.

'No! He'll tell you because it's the truth!'

'I hope so, Mr Jones. Now, how did you spend the day following your visit to the Fountains Hotel? The day Mrs Hargreaves and Mrs Trenchard disappeared?'

For the first time the eyes slid away. 'I had appointments in the morning. You can check. In the afternoon I had some paperwork piled up, so I was at home.'

'On your own?'

'Yes!' The eyes now were defiant. 'I just told you, I was working.'

'Yes, of course. Thank you, Mr Jones. We'll leave it there for the time being.' Kendrick masked his frustration with a smile, and DS Wetherhead intoned the coda and switched off the machine. 'Someone'll get you a cup of tea now and take your detailed statement of how you spent the crucial day. Then we'll be able to check with the people you say you saw. I'm going to have a chat with your friend Des.'

Across the corridor Des Wilkins looked sulky, sitting pale and upright at the formica-topped table, with the attendant PC standing against the wall by the door. When Kendrick and Wetherhead came in Wilkins elaborately failed to acknowledge their entry, although Kendrick was aware of a swift movement of the eyes before they returned to space.

Motioning to the PC to take himself off, and to Wetherhead to insert the tape, Kendrick sat down and studied Wilkins in a silence that eventually shortened the long-distance gaze to a defiant locking with his own. 'Well, Mr Wilkins,' Kendrick said then, 'I've had a chat with your mate Gary Jones and now I'm going to have a chat with you. All right, Sergeant.'

Wetherhead gave the tape the cast list and the time, and Kendrick made a show of relaxing his big body on the small, hard chair. Wilkins hadn't appeared to move a muscle, except one or two round his mouth which had fashioned it into a sneer. Regarding it, Kendrick had to take a grip on himself.

'So, Mr Wilkins,' he managed, amiably enough. 'You and your mate Gary Jones had a drink at the hotel where Mrs Hargreaves was staying the night before she was murdered. And you did so in the hope of seeing her and her friend Mrs Trenchard.'

'Yeah, that's right,' Wilkins agreed. His eyes were dark and deep-set, and it was harder than with Jones to be sure how they were reacting.

'Why did you want to see them?'

'Don't tell me you don't know, Chief Superintendent, I shan't believe you.'

'Just answer my question.' Kendrick was glad to see a tic at work under Wilkins' left eye, belying his air of impudent relaxation.

Des Wilkins shrugged. 'Okay. We wanted to see them because it was part of the ongoing joke we had at the art class. And it was the only opportunity we'd had—or were ever likely to have—of maybe getting them to have a drink with us.' Wilkins paused, and looked with a good imitation of a derisive smile from one policeman to the other. 'You can't be serious, Chief Superintendent, you can't be suggesting—'

'Gary Jones tells us he left the bar to go to the men's room. Did he take this with him?' Kendrick pushed the note across a table for the second time.

Des Wilkins had his face down over it for longer than it could have taken him to read it, but it came up smiling. 'You really have to be joking, Mr Kendrick. Did you write this yourself?'

'You'll come better out of this interview if you remain civil!' DS Wetherhead flashed, and Kendrick was glad to see Wilkins' first twitch of unease. He was also grateful to his sergeant for administering the reproof: his own version could have been much stronger.

'The note is genuine,' he told Wilkins coolly. 'And it was typed and printed in the leisure complex computer room. By you, Mr Wilkins?'

'Of course not!' But Des Wilkins was jolted at last, and the hand lying beside the note was trembling. Kendrick saw his adam's apple bob a couple of times before he spoke again. 'And d'you really think I'd've associated myself before a classful of people with someone I was blackmailing? Asked for her in a hotel?'

'You're a confident sort of fellow,' Kendrick said. 'I can see you responding to a dare with a load of adrenaline. So I think you might have done. Especially if you were confident the lady would keep quiet and pay up.'

'I never!' Wilkins was on his feet, and shouting.

'Sit down!' DS Wetherhead shouted in his turn, after a glance at Kendrick, and Wilkins obeyed. 'That's better. Now, we'll be asking you of course for a detailed written statement of your movements on the day the two ladies disappeared, but perhaps you'll give us a verbal outline now.'

'I'm a sales rep. Okay?' Wilkins was still holding up, but his narrow chest in the thin sweater was showing increasing evidence that he was breathing hard. 'Which makes it difficult to be exact. Calling on a client isn't like going into a meeting timed for ten, eleven o'clock. I was out and about most of the morning and'—wariness flashed noticeably across the eyes—'working at home most of the afternoon.'

'Anyone who can vouch for that?'

'No,' Wilkins said sullenly. 'And there wouldn't be. I told you, I was working.'

'Like your mate Gary. Of course. Thank you, Mr Wilkins.' Kendrick got to his feet, nodded to DS Wetherhead to terminate the interview, and turned back to the interviewee. 'Perhaps you'll be good enough now to give my sergeant a detailed statement of your movements during the day Mrs Hargreaves and Mrs Trenchard disappeared. Then we'll ask you and Mr Jones to accompany our officers to your homes while they have a look around.'

When Kendrick got back to his office he found DS Wetherhead waiting to tell him that Mrs Hargreaves had not taken five hundred pounds in cash out of her private or business accounts during the past month.

'The note refers to the "usual" meeting place, sir, so perhaps we can assume five hundred pounds is the same sum as on earlier occasions, but the lady's financial behaviour's so erratic it's impossible to tell when she may have paid other sums in the past, or of what size. She could have taken money out in bits, so that it didn't show.'

'She could, Fred. But what I'm glad you haven't told me is that she took a round five hundred pounds out shortly before her death. At least we can assume that this time the blackmailer was frustrated.' Although his sergeant's information had been negative, Kendrick was feeling at last that he was beginning to get somewhere.

Chapter Ten

Phyllida Moon was walking through a mistily beautiful seascape beside a large, kind-eyed man who made her feel happy. Her happiness kept coming out in laughter, and the other reason she was laughing was because the man was funny as well as kind. He was happy, too, and nothing needed to be said to explain their happiness.

But suddenly the world was darkening and she was afraid. She cried out, and the man took her hand. He said, 'It's all right, Phyllida!' and the light came back and it was. This time she cried out in relief and gratitude, so loudly she woke herself up.

Absurdly pleased that the man had called her by her own name, Phyllida ran to the window to open the curtains, then got into bed again and lay looking out at the scene which had been the backdrop of her dream. The deep curve of the bay facing the frilly white line of the grey water, outlined in parallel by an arc of pale sand and the white Victorian buildings, looked like a nineteenth century print, misty in reality at this early stage of the morning but no longer generating her dream awareness of infinite possibility.

But it did generate, at least, a view; for the last few days the outlook to which Phyllida had awakened had been the interior well of the Golden Lion Hotel, and it was good to be back in her own bed and able to look out at the elating sweep of sky and sea. Today was the day of the art class, and over their late chat and nightcap in the office the evening before, Peter had told her he thought she was perhaps giving too much time and attention to duty and it would be good preparation for the class to go home to sleep. None of her personae was expecting a call at the Golden

Lion, he reminded her, and Reception would tell anyone who rang that whoever they wanted was for the moment unavailable but to leave a name and number. Reception would then ring her at home—as, he reminded her farther, they had done a number of times in the past—and she could ring back when she was ready as if from the hotel with no threat to her anonymity: she had instructed British Telecom not to give her number to anyone dialling the service which would normally have revealed it.

'You've no other reason for sleeping at the Golden Lion just now, so take advantage,' Peter had urged. 'And in fact you don't have to go there at all until you're ready to turn into Fiona. It's too soon to call on Sally Hargreaves again and you don't have anything currently demanding in other directions, so go to the library as Phyllida Moon and work on your book. A few hours in your own persona could be ... helpful.'

Peter had paused before bringing out that last word, and Phyllida had wondered, not for the first time, if he was aware of the fragility of her sense of identity as well as of her growing concern for Sally Hargreaves.

Whatever his motive, she had found herself ready to accept his suggestions. But as she lay watching the featureless grey sky and seeing it slowly assume colours and contours, she discovered that she was too engrossed with the Hargreaves/Trenchard affair to be able to switch her attention to her own academic concerns. And by the time a pale sun had arced over Great Hill and turned it black above a suddenly pink-tinged sea, Phyllida knew that it was Miss Pym who would go to the library, and sit in the lending section at the spot she and Sally had approved. *Moths* would provide relaxation, but would not be distracting enough to prevent awareness of what was going on around her and any relevant chat. She would also, of course, have a word with whoever was in Sally's place and try to gauge public perception of the tragedy.

It was easy, then, to get up and dressed and out, and she had to force herself to sit for the five minutes it took to drink a mug of tea and eat a slice of toast. As she walked down the short slope of her road to the promenade Phyllida found that the print had been transformed into a watercolour, and marvelled yet again at the power of the sea to render a prospect volatile. Her love affair with the ocean, at least, would never grow stale.

By the time she arrived within the four severe walls of her hotel bedroom Phyllida was in an unfamiliar state of euphoria, which swelled even higher as she realized that it belonged to her and not to any of her characters. It took several glances down the well shaft and a talking to herself from a hard chair to bring her close enough to her usual state of blinkered professionalism to begin creating Miss Pym, but she was still uncharacteristically exhilarated as the old lady trotted downstairs and out, as Phyllida had come in, through the back door of the hotel in case Peter should be doing some thinking by his window and see her disobeying him.

At first, when she entered the library's lending section and looked towards the central desk, Phyllida thought she had been unlucky: there was no sign of Stephen, and in a temporary absence of clientele the young woman behind the counter was attending absorbedly to her nails, an activity, in Phyllida's experience, which did not augur well for a girl's attention to the job for which she was paid.

But as Miss Pym diffidently approached the desk the nail file was whisked out of sight and an older and potentially more helpful woman appeared from the other side of the circle. She greeted the old lady with a smile before frowning towards the girl, now apparently absorbed in a stack of print-outs.

'Can I help you?' the woman asked as she sat down beside the computer.

'Well, I think so,' Miss Pym responded diffidently. 'Miss Hargreaves . . . poor Miss Hargreaves'—the older woman nodded sympathetically and the younger looked up sharply from the print-outs, a brief gleam in her eye—'was keeping a book for me under the counter. Just where you're sitting,' Miss Pym went on apologetically. 'It's heavy and I only read it here, so she said she would keep it for me and let me have it when I came in. I'm Miss Agnes Pym and it's called—'

'*Moths*!' the senior woman interrupted, handing the book over with another smile. 'Just sit down wherever you like, Miss Pym, and do some more reading.'

'Thank you, you're very kind. How . . . how is Sally? I thought she might be back but—oh, dear!—it's so very terrible. Is she all right?'

'I went to see her yesterday. No, she isn't all right, of course, but she's trying to bear up.' The woman glanced round the quiet room. 'It looks as though the media have taken themselves off, so I should think she'll be back before long, she told me she'd rather be working than brooding at home.'

'Yes, I'm sure . . . Poor Sally! Have they—are the police anywhere near making an arrest? I'm afraid I'm always out of date with the news and I was wondering . . .'

'Sally didn't say much, but she didn't give me the impression the police had anyone in their sights.'

The younger woman was languidly answering a query and there was another customer waiting beside Miss Pym. 'Well,' the old lady said, 'I'll go and read my book now and let you get on. Is Stephen in today?'

'Not today, he's on a course.'

'I see. Thank you.'

She'd give it an hour, Phyllida decided as she sat down. It looked as though she had learned all she was going to learn, and it hadn't been of any significance . . .

'Miss Pym?'

Miss Pym jumped and gave a little squeak of shock, because Phyllida, in her unwarranted disappointment, had for the last few moments turned her full attention on to *Moths*. She looked up into the face of the tall young man who was bending over her. Its anxiety was so intense she was aware of it well before she was aware of his unshowy good looks.

'Yes, I'm Miss Agnes Pym. How can I help you?'

'Well . . . May I sit down?' The young man indicated the other chair at the table without taking his suppliant eyes from Miss Pym's face. 'It's important,' he went on in a rush. 'It's about Sally.'

Phyllida let her own face light up. The luck Peter was convinced was an ingredient of every case had come her way. But she had set it up—a piece of ammunition with which to attack him in the future when he told her to take it a bit easy. 'Sally! Oh!' Miss Pym's voice, to Phyllida's distaste, had become slightly arch. 'I have an idea you're Jeremy!'

'I am, yes.' A brief but attractive smile had interrupted the anxiety. 'Look, could we have a coffee while I talk to you? I'm so worried, you see.'

'Yes, I can see,' Miss Pym said, regarding him. 'And of course you can talk to me, Jeremy. I may call you Jeremy?' He nodded, trying, and almost succeeding, to keep impatience out of his second smile. 'Very well, let us go.'

Miss Pym handed *Moths* back to the older woman behind the counter, told her she didn't think she would want it again that day, and walked with Jeremy Clark's hand at her elbow out of the lending library and across the marbled hall to the café, dotted with small white-clothed tables and bentwood chairs. Phyllida had been going there for tea and coffee breaks from her concentration in the reference library ever since her arrival in Seaminster the previous summer as a member of the Independent Theatre Company, and it felt friendly and familiar. All the more friendly, perhaps, she reflected ruefully as she settled into a chair and watched Jeremy Clark walk over to the long counter, because it had been a means of postponing her return to Gerald.

'Here you go!' Jeremy took a coffee and a home-made biscuit from the tray he was carrying and set them in front of her, then did the same for himself. 'Now,' he said, as he slid the tray on to an empty table and sat down, 'you must be wondering, Miss Pym, why on earth I've accosted you.'

'Well yes, of course, and I'm hoping it may be because you think I can help you in some way. I'm so concerned about Sally, you know. Forgive me,' Miss Pym went on immediately, 'that must sound arrogant. My anxiety can only be a shadow of yours, but Sally and I made friends very easily and I feel I've known her for far longer than I have.'

'That's exactly how Sally feels!' Jeremy Clark took up eagerly.

His eagerness, his floppy hair and his sensitive features made Phyllida think of a darker version of Peter. 'She told me so. So I decided to look for you. I only had the library to go on, and it's such a relief to have made goal on my first try. Gosh, sorry, that was a bit of a crude way of putting it!' He smiled apologetically, what Phyllida saw as natural good manners for a moment overcoming his anxiety.

'Graphic, none the less,' Miss Pym conceded. 'Now, Jeremy, please tell me what you think I can do for you.'

For the first time he hesitated, running a long index finger through a mound of spilled sugar. 'It's going to sound ridiculous put into words,' he said eventually. 'But . . . ever since this unspeakable thing happened I've felt . . . I've felt that Sally knows something about it, something she can't or won't—tell anyone. Even me. And I think if she *did* tell anyone it *would* be me. I'm not suggesting of course that she's told *you*, but she said how intelligent you are—which I can see for myself, of course—and I just wondered if she might have let something slip, or you might have got some idea . . .'

'Yes,' Miss Pym said decidedly, after a short pause of her own. 'I *did* feel there was something.' Phyllida paused again. She had to appear to be searching her memory, she couldn't bring out pat the words she had quoted in her report and which she knew by heart. 'She seemed so certain her mother and her friend weren't going to an—an assignation. So very certain, it made me wonder if she knew what they *were* doing.'

'That's exactly what I felt!' In his excitement Jeremy Clark had raised his voice and banged the table, and he looked round the sparsely populated room with a sheepish grin. 'And I've felt,' he went on quietly, 'several times, that she was about to tell me something, then drew back.'

'I didn't feel she was going to tell me anything, of course,' Miss Pym said, 'although she said she was finding it surprisingly easy to talk to someone she didn't know. So perhaps . . .'

'She's decided to go back to work tomorrow,' he said, anxious again. 'So, d'you think . . . Could you go and see her this afternoon?

I know she'd be pleased, she told me she hoped she'd see you again soon. Could you? She just might . . .'

'Of course I'll go!' Miss Pym assured him. 'When you get to my age there's not much you can do for people and I'm grateful for an opportunity. You mustn't let yourself get excited, though, Jeremy. But I might get some idea even if she doesn't actually tell me anything.'

'You just might, I suspect,' he said, looking into her eyes and grinning. 'Thank you for being willing to try.' He dropped his eyes to the table and began to reassemble the sugar mound. 'Could I just ask you before we go our separate ways . . . Is there anything else you can remember from your first visit?'

Phyllida had been thinking while Miss Pym talked. 'Once or twice she looked, well, *bewildered*. As if there was something she couldn't understand. Something apart from the awful fact of the murder, I mean. And . . .' Phyllida paused to make it seem Miss Pym was still considering. 'When I asked her if her mother and her friend had told her anything about what they planned to do that day she said no readily enough, but she looked away from me and her face went very white. I remember being afraid she was about to faint.'

'So I haven't been imagining things!'

'Perhaps not.' Phyllida wished Miss Pym knew about the blackmail note. 'Is she close to her father?'

'Yes. They're very good friends.'

'But you don't think she's said anything to him? You haven't seen anything in his manner to suggest it?'

'I should say *not*,' Jeremy responded promptly. 'I think I get on well with Matthew'—Phyllida warmed to the diffidence—'and I'm pretty sure I'd have noticed if his manner had changed since Carol's death. Well, of course it's changed, he's devastated, but he hasn't shown that extra thing Sally's shown. Shown right from the start. In fact . . .' Jeremy paused, looking earnestly at Miss Pym. 'I haven't told you the most fanciful part yet,' he said.

'But please do. It might make my visit this afternoon more helpful.'

'Yes, of course. It's just that it sounds ... Miss Pym, the night Carol and Maggie came to dinner at the flat—the last night of their lives—I got home later than I'd intended—an unexpected client—and I found the three of them, Carol, Maggie and Sally ... well, they seemed to be in a state of euphoria. I'd have said they'd been drinking, only so little of our own drink had gone down and the bottle of wine Carol and Maggie had brought hadn't been opened. But they were all sort of—over the top. To such an extent Maggie had a turn and had to go and lie down. Miss Pym, with Maggie it took so little ... She must have seen ...'

'Don't,' Miss Pym urged softly, putting her hand for an instant on his as she saw his face distort.

'I try not to.' Jeremy Clark shook his head and tried to smile. 'Anyway. Sally's—strangeness—started then, as soon as her mother and Maggie left. Before the murders. When we'd seen them off I said they'd all seemed to be in exceptional spirits and when she said yes, well, they were on holiday she didn't meet my eyes, and she hasn't always met them since. It's nothing to do with her and me,' Jeremy assured Miss Pym. 'We're fine. But there's this area where, well, where I don't feel she's being honest with me, where I feel she's holding something back.'

'I think I understand, Jeremy. I'm just sorry I haven't been more helpful.'

'But you've been very helpful! You've shown me I'm not imagining it. And perhaps this afternoon ... Gosh, I'm mucking up your day, aren't I?'

'Not in the least. As I've just told you, I welcome the rare opportunities I get to be useful. If I have anything to tell you, shall I ring you at your office?' If there was anything to tell she would tell it to Peter, and tell Jeremy Clark she had drawn a blank, which she didn't look forward to. If only the murderer could be found Miss Pym could follow her earlier creations into oblivion before she had to disappoint him, but this was hardly likely in the time available. And when Miss Pym did disappear, Phyllida would, for the first time, insist on some sort of explanation to the people one of her characters had got to know ...

She pulled her mind back to the present. Jeremy Clark was smiling as he thanked Miss Pym, then looking anxious again. 'You won't tell Sally, will you, that we've had this conversation? That we've met?'

'Of course not,' Miss Pym responded truthfully. 'And I hope none of Sally's colleagues will, either. Do they know you?'

'One or two. The ones I saw this morning were strangers.'

'Good. And even if someone you know *did* see you and tells Sally, they won't tell her before my visit this afternoon.'

'You're on the ball, Miss Pym,' Jeremy said admiringly.

'Maybe. Now, I think I'll go home and have a little rest before this afternoon. You're sure Sally will be in?'

'I'm sure. She told me this morning she'd postpone the big bad world until tomorrow. But I suspect you'd prefer to ring her than to arrive unheralded.' He glanced at his watch. 'Oh, Lord, I've a client in ten minutes.'

They parted outside the library, and both Miss Pym and Phyllida looked approvingly after Jeremy Clark as he hurtled away. Phyllida telephoned Sally the moment she was back in her room at the Golden Lion, and was rapturously received.

'I'm going back to the library tomorrow, Miss Pym. Thank goodness!'

'I'm so glad, Sally. I was going to suggest coming to see you this afternoon, but perhaps as it's your last afternoon—'

'I'd love you to come and see me!' Sally interrupted. 'As soon as I heard your voice I wanted to ask you, but you're so kind I was afraid you'd say yes when you really wanted to rest or something. About three?'

'I rest too much of the time. I'll see you about three.' She shouldn't need, or be expected, to stay beyond an hour, so there would be plenty of time before the art class both to visit the Agency and to assume Fiona's identity. And Phyllida had already discovered that it was easier to go from one character to another without the intervention of herself.

Phyllida took off Miss Pym's sensible shoes and her hat, and got on to the bed before lifting the telephone. Jenny told her both Peter and Steve were out.

'That's all right, I just wanted to leave a message. Will you tell Peter that Miss Pym's going to see Sally Hargreaves again this afternoon? I rang to see how she was and discovered she's going back to work tomorrow, so it's maybe the last opportunity to see her in private. I'll come straight to the Agency when I leave her.' Phyllida paused. 'You can also tell him if you will, Jenny, that I'll be resting until the afternoon's assignment.' Which wasn't a lie, she'd be having a cat nap in a minute, although she had given the impression that she was ringing from home.

The nap, followed by a lunch of coffee and sandwiches brought up to the room and a few chapters of a crime novel, took her agreeably to the time to refresh Miss Pym and set out. As she left the hotel by the front door Phyllida glanced across the square at the Agency, content now for Peter to see her: she had told Jenny Miss Pym was visiting Sally Hargreaves, and he knew that she never left her own home in disguise.

There was no one at any of the Agency windows, and no representative of the media outside the block of flats where Sally was awaiting her. Sally's voice sounded less scared than it had sounded the first time she had answered the buzzer, but when she reached the third floor and saw the girl awaiting her in her doorway, Phyllida was shocked by the change in her appearance since they had last met. Sally's eyes now were enormous and the planes of her face shockingly apparent. What should have been snugly fitting jeans were loose round her narrow thighs, and her lustrous hair looked dull and dry. Phyllida had to check her own dismay before dressing it up as Miss Pym's.

'Sally, dear, you don't look at all well!' she said, as Sally shut the door behind her.

'No, well, I'm not sleeping much at the moment, and I don't seem to be hungry.'

'Are you sure you're up to going back to work tomorrow?' Miss Pym inquired anxiously, as she took the edge of the chair she had taken on her first visit.

'I've got to go back!' Sally said wearily, as she slumped down opposite. 'I can't stay brooding here on my own any longer. I'm getting so *dull*, Miss Pym, I'm sure Jeremy's going to start feeling . . . He's so good and kind and patient, but I'm in a dark hole and I can't climb out of it. He's bound to get fed up.'

'I'm sure he won't, Sally, But perhaps it will help *you*, to be among other people. You have to eat though, child, you really do, however little you want to, or you'll make yourself physically ill and that won't be any good to anyone. Are you listening to me?' Miss Pym asked in mock severity, and Phyllida was relieved to see a brief smile.

'I am, Miss Pym, and I know you're right. Look, I'll put the kettle on, and then you can watch me eat a biscuit. All right?'

'Certainly, Sally. And it will be better still if Jeremy sees you eating some dinner tonight. Will you try?'

'I'll try.' Sally smiled again, and her step as she went out of the room was less weary than when she had entered it.

'How are your father and Mr Trenchard?' Miss Pym asked, when Sally had returned with a tray, poured tea, and swallowed half a biscuit.

'At least they're back at work. They're devastated, but Daddy's taking it better than Frank, somehow. I'm a bit worried about Frank.'

'I hope you're seeing your father regularly, Sally.'

'Oh, yes, he comes to dinner, and we'll be together at the weekend. He's not staying with Frank now, he's gone home.' Sally paused. 'He's there on his own. I've let him down.'

'What do you mean, dear?'

'I mean I can't go back to the house. I can't keep him company or see that he and everything else at home are all right. I keep asking him to come and stay here for as long as he likes, but he wants to be at home and I can't be!'

'That's understandable.'

'No it isn't!' Sally shouted. 'It's beastly cowardly, it makes me ashamed of myself, it makes me disgusted. But I still can't do it.'

'Perhaps in a little while—'

'I don't know. Oh, God ...' Sally had been twisting about in her chair, but she was suddenly still, and her eyes were fixed hypnotically on Phyllida's as she leaned slowly forward, her pale thin hands dangling between her knees. 'Miss Pym, may I talk.to you about something? Something I haven't talked to anyone else about?'

'Of course, dear. But Jeremy ... Your father ...?' Phyllida suggested reluctantly. 'Shouldn't it be Jeremy or your father you talk to?'

'No!' Sally screwed her face up as if she was in physical pain. 'I can't talk to *them*, they're suffering too much, I can only talk to someone who isn't—part of it.'

'All right, Sally.' Phyllida's fingers itched for pen and paper. 'Tell me, if it will help.'

'Thank you.'

Sally got up and stood with her forehead against the window, then suddenly whirled round. 'Miss Pym, when I—when I—' She stopped abruptly and dropped into a chair with a long sigh. 'The police found a note in Mummy's pocket,' she said, after a moment's silence. 'Asking her to hand over some money if she didn't want Daddy to be told what she'd been up to.'

'Oh, Sally! But surely ... surely you and your father and Jeremy have talked about *that*?' Phyllida knew she had been within an ace of learning something she didn't already know, and felt sick with frustration and disappointment.

'Not really. It's too awful. When the Chief Superintendent told us about it and asked us if we knew what it was referring to Daddy said of course he didn't, and that no one could ever persuade him his darling'—Sally choked on a sob—'had been doing anything bad. And he said that to Frank, and to Jeremy. And to me of course. Thank heaven the police aren't telling the media. But they've found out that the note was printed on a computer at the leisure complex, and so they'll be questioning people at the art class—Frank says they're bound to, especially those two men Mummy and Maggie used to laugh about—and somebody there could let it out. Oh, Miss Pym, I hope they don't! I hope ...'

'Yes, Sally?'

'I hope they find the fiend who killed my mother. And Maggie, who was killed by seeing Mummy die.'

'Do you have any idea what the note could have been referring to, Sally?'

'Of course not, it wasn't referring to anything! The murderer wrote it because it wasn't enough for him to take Mummy's life, he wanted her reputation too.' But Sally's face was dead white and her eyes were no longer meeting Phyllida's.

Chapter Eleven

'I felt that another tête-à-tête might do it,' Phyllida told Peter, when she had talked out her frustration. 'So I took a shot to nothing. Miss Pym told Sally just before she left that she was being turned out from her cousin's boarding house for the summer as usual and had to find somewhere else to live. You know what happens at the seaside, the terms go up after Easter and the impecunious winter residents have to look for other accommodation until the autumn.'

'I know.'

'Well, Miss Pym asked Sally if she knew of a suitable and reasonable guest house, and Sally said she'd enquire and meanwhile Miss Pym was to move into the flat. In fact she would *like* Miss Pym to move into the flat because Jeremy was about to start a job that would take him away overnight for a spell. I'd already discovered that the guest bedroom has an en-suite bathroom. Peter?'

'Does whisky inhibit your powers of transformation?'

'I shouldn't think so, in moderation.'

'Right.' Peter opened the small disguised filing cabinet and poured into a couple of glasses.

'Is this to toast my enterprise?' Phyllida enquired as she took one. 'Or to soften the blow of refusal?'

'To toast your enterprise, I'm afraid,' Peter said apologetically. 'I probably ought to be refusing you, but I'm not going to.'

'Kendrick may.'

'I doubt it, but I'll contact him in the morning. When do you propose to move in?'

'Saturday afternoon, by taxi. Sally's invited Miss Pym to join the family for lunch on Sunday, and on Monday I'll be able to look round the flat when she's at work, see if she's put any of her knowledge in written form. It's tacky, but it's her mother's murder. I'll find some excuse to leave on Tuesday, unless something happens that indicates I should stay longer.'

'Will you be able to sustain the make-up for so long at such close quarters?'

'If I feel uneasy about it, Miss Pym will have a turn and go and lie down alone in a darkened room.'

'You're an extraordinary woman.'

'I don't think so.' Phyllida could not imagine any woman more ordinary than herself.

'Talking of Kendrick. Our Chief Superintendent has a message for Miss Bowden. Don't look so worried. His minions have done some homework. Miss Elizabeth Cummings partakes of fish and chips at Robinson's Café round the corner from the leisure complex at six-thirty p.m. before she attends the art class. I hope you haven't eaten?'

'Mrs Steele will be able to manage a sandwich. That was clever of the minions, wasn't it, Peter?'

'Not quite so clever when you've already discovered that she attends two more classes at the complex—cookery and dressmaking—on two other nights of the week, and eats at Robinson's each time. Now, Kendrick wasn't suggesting Miss Cummings humped two dead bodies on to a traffic island, but he did think that to have a private chat with her about her views on her fellow members of the art class just might be useful.'

'So it might.' The adrenaline was flowing and Phyllida got to her feet, handing Peter her empty glass. 'I'd better get into Fiona.'

'Right. I got hold of Trenchard earlier on, and ended up with an invitation to his house tonight, where Hargreaves is going to be. When Kendrick rang about you and Miss Cummings he told me that what's left of the dead women has been released, so perhaps I'll discover the funeral date. If it isn't arranged yet, Miss Pym may be luckier.'

Robinson's Café was rather what Phyllida had expected from her short acquaintance with Miss Cummings. Seaminster was known for its charming and idiosyncratic eating places, but Robinson's was not one of them. Glaringly lit even on a bright spring evening by ranks of overhead fluorescent tubes, its bumpy unadorned walls an overall buttercup yellow, its tables topped with blue formica and its chairs anchored pairs of moulded plastic, it was totally functional. So anodyne was its exterior that Phyllida was halfway past it when she saw Miss Cummings ensconced in the window corner, already broaching a piled plateful of chips and a wedge of battered fish.

At least the place was clean, and the smell of frying with which Phyllida was immediately assailed was wholesome. When she turned towards the window Miss Cummings had her knife and fork pointing ceilingwards and her eyes fixed anxiously on Mrs Steele. Braced for the usual cool reception but hoping for better, Phyllida guessed, with a brief stab of pity. Miss Cummings' hair looked more perm-defeated than ever, and under the harsh light her face was strained and pale. As Fiona mimed recognition the hovering smile settled on her lips and she put her knife and fork down.

Phyllida took the few steps necessary to reach hailing distance. 'Hello!' she said, in surprise. 'We have the same idea.'

'The haddock's excellent!' Miss Cummings announced. She had a light, rather high voice which Phyllida already knew could become petulant. 'Join me if you'd like to when you've ordered.'

'Thank you. I will.'

As Fiona turned away with a smile Phyllida reflected almost guiltily on how easy it was to be kind to lame dogs when you knew you wouldn't have to keep it up. The acting she was doing now brought in its train a host of moral ambiguities that had been absent from the acting she had done all her adult life on stage, where everyone was in on the charade and the real world was totally excluded. It was the mingling of the two worlds, the fictional and the real, she realised as she took her place at the end of the short queue, the pretences made to people who didn't know she was pretending, that made the work she was doing now so uneasy as well as so seductive . . .

'Yes?'

At the last moment Phyllida found she couldn't entirely oblige Miss Cummings. 'A cheese and tomato sandwich, please, on brown, and a black coffee.'

The sandwich, enclosed in plastic, was put instantly on to a plate, and the coffee immediately followed.

'That won't take you far,' Miss Cummings sniffed, as Fiona arrived at her table.

'I had a full lunch,' Fiona explained. 'So I only want a snack.'

'Oh. You'll have to try the haddock sometime, it's very good.'

'I'm sure.' Miss Cummings was eyeing her obliquely, the smile gone and both caution and disapproval in her pale eyes. Ideological disapproval of an attractive woman? 'Those two ladies from the class who I never met,' Fiona said as she wrestled with the sandwich pack. 'I don't remember what Mrs Elliot said their names were, but from what I've read . . . They *are* the two ladies whose bodies were found on the roundabout?'

'Yes.' Miss Cummings had taken the pack out of Phyllida's fingers and had her head down as she opened it with one expert movement. 'There you are.' She put it back in front of Phyllida. 'Terrible, isn't it?' But her eyes as they met Phyllida's were excited.

'Thank you. Yes, it's terrible. Especially when you actually *knew* them. I had a drink with those two young men and Mr Pusey after the class last week and Mr Pusey said how nice they were. I gathered it was all a bit of a joke, the business of the two men being devastated by their absence and so on . . .'

Another sniff. 'That's what everyone thought, and it would certainly have been hard to believe . . . But women like that, who knows?'

'Like what?' Fiona asked with interest. 'According to the press they were happily married and had never been in any sort of trouble—'

'There's trouble and there's trouble!' And there was venom, too, bringing brief animation to Miss Cummings' face and voice. 'Those two women were flirts, they encouraged the men's ridiculous behaviour—d'you think they'd have gone on being so silly, week after week, if they'd had no encouragement? Glances, smiles, ways of walking . . . Women like that ask for it!'

'To be murdered?'

Miss Cummings' face and neck flooded an unattractive shade of pink.

'Of course not,' she muttered, dropping her eyes to her plate. 'But if you play with fire . . .'

'That's putting it a bit strongly, surely? Someone from the class, though, is going to tell the police about the charade the men played. It could be awkward for them.'

'And so it should be!'

'Even if they're innocent?' Fiona asked.

Miss Cummings looked up sharply 'I wasn't saying . . . If those two women behaved like that in the class, they'll have behaved like that away from it! They'll have made fools of other men! But men are fools anyway.'

'I thought some of the men in the art class seemed quite bright,' Fiona said. 'But you wouldn't agree with me?'

'The old gentlemen are all right,' Miss Cummings said grudgingly. 'Quite courteous and considerate.'

'The man who makes everyone laugh really is funny.'

'Making a joke of everything?'

'It wasn't my impression that he did that. I just thought he seemed to have a good slant on life.'

'He's all right,' Miss Cummings opined, grudgingly again. 'Which is more than can be said for that dreadful creature with the eyes. I'm sure he's not all there.'

'Yes, I know who you mean. You're somehow always aware of him, moving around.'

'He does it on purpose, you know,' Miss Cummings said. 'Stamping about, knocking into things. No one's allowed to smoke in the class, of course, but he sticks a dead pipe in his mouth sometimes as if it's a dummy, and once he actually knocked it out on the side of my chair and the ash went all over my drawing. He didn't apologize, he just walked away.'

'That must have been infuriating,' Phyllida said, in genuine sympathy. *And the behaviour of a psychopath?* She must beware the cuddly bunny syndrome, but she felt she would be in order to include Miss Cummings' anecdote in her report. That big man—Mr Pusey, isn't it?—looks like a decent chap.'

'Oh, him.'

'You don't like him, Miss Cummings?'

'I don't trust him. Enough said.'

'Of course.' Phyllida tried to banish an unprofessional pang of unease. 'I should think everyone likes the young man. He has bags of charm.'

'He was always making up to the Hargreaves woman. Saying how wonderful she was at designing book jackets.'

'Someone told me he'd lost his job and was interested in learning about jacket design.'

Miss Cummings shrugged, then suddenly and accusingly fixed her eyes on Phyllida. 'There are women in the class as well as men, you know.'

'Yes, of course. I think you have a friend there, don't you, Miss Cummings?'

'Oh, Ida. Yes.'

'Do you sometimes eat together beforehand?'

'Very rarely. Ida insists she can't afford it. But we're on the same bus route and we take it in turns afterwards to provide the cocoa.'

'That's nice,' Phyllida responded, suppressing a shudder. But at least she wasn't having to parry questions about herself; Miss Cummings had already proved she was uninterested in other people unless their behaviour affected her.

'Those two men who made up to the murdered women,' Miss Cummings said, swallowing her last mouthful. 'I don't think we can expect to see them tonight.'

'No?'

'Feeling too stupid, and probably at the police station anyway.'

'I suppose the police will have to question them.' Phyllida reminded herself that only those members of the class whom the police chose to interview would be aware of the existence of the note. 'But they'll hardly suspect them of murdering Mrs Hargreaves just because she didn't respond to them.'

'Maybe she did.' Miss Cummings poured a last thin trickle of dark tea and drank it down. Then looked at her watch. 'Have you finished? We ought to be on our way.'

'Fine.' There was plenty of time, but Miss Cummings was the type of person who is always anxious to arrive early. And Phyllida herself was eager for the heady atmosphere of an art studio.

As anticipated, Des Wilkins and Gary Jones failed to put in an appearance, and she was dismayed by the jolt of mingled relief and apprehension that went through her when Jack Pusey walked through the door. His face was grave, but his eyes roved the room until they found her, and then he smiled. Phyllida smiled back before turning on a professional reflex to where Miss Cummings, just behind her, was arranging her easel.

She was rewarded. Miss Cummings was looking at Jack Pusey with what Phyllida could interpret only as a passionate longing, a look that sat bizarrely on her prim, bloodless features. Passionate, though, with love or loathing? Phyllida realised on another jolt that her job as well as her inclinations demanded a tête-à-tête with Jack, and was ruefully amused by the confidence with which Fiona anticipated that he would suggest one.

But first the class must acknowledge the tragedy which had befallen two of its members so that they could put it behind them. Phyllida's sympathy for Mrs Elliot at having to take the lead soon turned to admiration of the delicate aplomb with which she met the task. Dressed appropriately in generously cut floor-length black culottes under a black blouse diagonally slashed with purple, she stood in the midst of her students like a priestess among her congregation, the nucleus of their mourning. It was only when she had concluded her short, surprisingly unemotive announcement, decreed and gained a short silence, and moved on to her usual opening position in front of the blackboards that she told them matter-of-factly that Des Wilkins and Gary Jones had telephoned to say they were unable to get to the class that night. It was a measure of her command of the collective mood, Phyllida thought, that there was no audible reaction.

The mourning ceremony offered Phyltrda a good opportunity to observe the members of the class reacting to it: George the joker looking rueful and examining a fingernail; the two ladies at the table wearing identical expressions of sorrowful disapproval on their well-bred, well-painted faces; the old men with their heads bowed; Miss Cummings and her lookalike exchanging glances of smug understanding; the man with the piercing eyes punctuating Mrs Elliot's discourse with regular sharp rasping noises—the shuffle of his feet, his hands on his easel, the scrape of his chair; one of the young girls with tears on her face being comforted by the other; young Paul Denton crying, too, quietly, tears running down his cheeks; and Jack Pusey, calm, grave, attentive ... None of it amounted to anything significant in the context of the murder, but Phyllida would put it in her report because there was unlikely to be anything else.

She spent an hour of happiness colourwashing her still life, then joined the straggle out to the corridor for coffee.

'Fiona!'

The warm, deep voice she had been expecting sounded behind her almost immediately and she turned round. 'Hello, Jack. Gary and Des aren't ill, I hope?'

'No.' He had a paper cup of coffee in either hand and gave her one without comment, which meant he had remembered she had had coffee last time rather than tea or orange juice. 'Just—not feeling up to it tonight.' Their eyes exchanged understanding. 'I hope their absence won't prevent you joining me for a drink afterwards?'

'I should like that. Thank you.' She wanted to go on looking at him, but she must look at other people. 'Will you excuse me now, though, I have to—'

'Of course.' He turned away, and feeling briefly chilly Phyllida went across to Paul Denton, who was standing alone and a little apart from the huddle round the drink machines.

'I'm so sorry,' she said quietly. 'I know you and Mrs Hargreaves were friends. I'm Fiona Steele.'

'Thank you. I'm Paul Denton. Well, if you know I knew Mrs Hargreaves, you'll know that, too.' The voice was soft and attractive, and Phyllida could see fine lines in the thin handsome face which made Paul Denton look older than he looked at a distance. 'She designs—*designed*'—Phyllida thought there was pain in the dark eyes as Denton corrected himself—'book jackets, and had just introduced me to her agent. I'm a commercial artist but I lost my last job.'

'I hope something comes of it.'

'Yes, but what a waste!' he said in sudden anger. 'She was so lovely and so talented.'

'And Mrs Trenchard . . .?'

'Mrs Trenchard too.' A tear escaped the suddenly sparkling eyes and rolled down his cheek. 'I still can't believe it,' he said fiercely. 'It's like a bad dream.'

'Everyone tells me how happy both of them were,' Phyllida said.

'They were!' he said. 'I'm sure they were. Well, Carol at any rate, I didn't really know Mrs Trenchard. We talked a lot about all sorts of things and she never gave me the least idea there was anything—well, anything wrong anywhere.'

'There probably wasn't. There so often isn't when you read in the press about awful things like this. There seems to be so much of it nowadays and usually when the police catch the criminals they look so very ordinary.'

'Sometimes.' Paul Denton stared towards the classroom door, and following his gaze Phyllida saw that it was on the man with the piercing eyes, who was standing in the doorway with his dead pipe in his mouth getting in the way of the people who were starting to move back to their work. 'It's nice of you to speak to me,' Denton said, bringing his eyes back to Phyllida. 'I appreciate it. I hope you enjoy the class despite what's happened.'

'Thank you.' Phyllida smiled and walked over to George the joker, also standing alone. 'We have need of you at the moment,' she told him, with another Fiona smile.

'Oh.' He looked away from her, embarrassed, and Phyllida thought she recognized the type: impersonally relaxed and fluent, embarrassed by one-to-one contact unless it was tried and trusted. 'I'm sorry,' she said, 'I didn't mean to make you self-conscious, I just wanted to tell you that I like your sense of humour.'

'Not very appropriate at the moment, is it?' With an effort he had looked back at her, and seemed a little reassured by the kindness of Fiona's smile.

Phyllida realised that during the first half of the evening he had been silent. 'It will be.'

'Thanks,' he said, smiling at last. Next time they came face to face he wouldn't look away from her.

Phyllida edged into the restrained lamentations of the two smart ladies, and as they widened into a general, 'What is the world coming to,' excused herself and went back into the studio.

'May I see what you've been doing?' Jack asked from behind her, as she reached her desk.

'I suppose so. I saw what you were doing last week. And liked it.'

'Thanks. I like this,' he said, when he had studied the still life for a few moments. 'You're not a beginner.'

'I felt like one last week, I haven't drawn or painted for years. It's a good feeling to be doing it again.'

Miss Cummings also had returned to her base, and was staring at Jack and Fiona with an intense expression Phyllida was unable to interpret.

'Hello!' Fiona said easily. 'May we look at your work, too?'

'If you wish.' Phyllida decided that Miss Cummings was angry, but as her gaze flickered between herself and Jack it was impossible to gauge whether it was with him, with Fiona, or with life in general.

The copy of a postcard of a cottage in a flower garden, originally painted by Miles Birkett Foster, had not improved from the week before.

'Very nice,' Jack said quickly, and Fiona murmured agreement.

'Thank you! It's fun to do.' But the enthusiasm Phyllida had been aware of in the moment of first meeting Miss Cummings had disappeared into the anger.

'It is indeed,' Jack said kindly, then turned to Fiona. 'I'll see you later,' he told her before walking away.

Miss Cummings stared after him, stared at Fiona, turned her eyes on to her painting.

'That's a nice man, you know,' Fiona said lightly.

'Is it?' Miss Cummings didn't look up.

By the end of the evening Phyllida had taken her still life as far as she and Mrs Elliot thought it should go, and felt a glow of achievement. With Miss Cummings sitting conveniently to the front and side of her, she had been able to look at her with no more than a slight movement of her head and a minimal disturbance of the artistic concentration for which, following so fruitful an evening, she had very little guilty conscience. To look at Fiona, Miss Cummings must turn round, but twice Phyllida's glance had met the angry glare. When Fiona said goodnight Jack was beside her, and Miss Cummings looked wordlessly from one to to the other before flouncing out.

Which made it easy to comment, although Phyllida held back until she and Jack were tucked into a corner of the Dog and Duck.

'Miss Cummings . . .' Fiona said then. 'She's a strange woman. I met her in a café before the class. She seemed to have as many chips on her shoulder as on her plate.'

Phyllida liked his laugh, and joined in. 'I can't see you in Robinson's,' Jack said when they had finished.

'A sudden impulse for a cup of coffee,' Fiona excused herself. 'But Miss Cummings . . . I thought she seemed *angry*. Not so much in the café, but in the break when she was talking to us both. I couldn't decide whether it was with me or with you, or with life in generaL'

'All three, perhaps,' Jack responded after a pause. 'Oh, dear!' He gave her a rueful smile, and although the light was dim she thought his complexion was suddenly more red than russet.

'What is it?'

'I was nice to her a few classes ago, I got her a coffee and gave her proper answers to some of the questions she asked me. I didn't make an excuse to leave her like I've noticed other people doing. And after that ...'

'Yes?'

'She starting asking me more questions, one of which was would I like the second ticket she had for a concert in the town hall. When she asked that question she put her hand on my arm ... That was the point when I told her, lightly and laughingly, that my wife wouldn't like it.'

'With Miss Cummings,' Phyllida managed, 'that would surely be enough.'

'Oh, yes, it was. Although not with a very good grace. And now, you see, I've left the class with another woman. But perhaps I'm being arrogant again and she's upset about something that has nothing to do with me at all'

'She was very disapproving of Mrs Hargreaves and Mrs Trenchard, she thought they were encouraging your friends Des and Gary.'

'Yes, she would.'

Phyllida sipped her wine. 'Des and Gary will be feeling upset. I suppose that's why they didn't come tonight.'

'Yes.'

Phyllida waited a few anxious seconds before carrying the conversation on. She would not think well of Jack Pusey if he told a comparative stranger about his friends' involvement with the police, and when he smiled at her in silence she was aware of an absurd sense of relief.

'It *was* a joke, though, wasn't it, Jack?'

'It was a joke, yes, but they really did think those two ladies were something.'

'Were they?'

'Yes. They *were* ladies for a start, they looked good, and they were nice. It's a wicked waste.'

'Mrs Elliot handled it well. Oh, I am *so* enjoying painting again!' She didn't know whether she had spoken professionally, to generalise the conversation, or because she had wanted to tell him that.

'What made you stop?'

'I don't know, really,' Phyllida said slowly. This was one of the areas where she and Fiona overlapped. 'I suppose I was doing—other things. Once you stop doing something, for whatever reason, it can be hard to start again, however much you enjoyed it.'

'You mustn't stop again. Are you feeling better?'

'Yes. Seaminster was a good idea. I'm happiest by the sea, I've decided.'

'So you'll have to come again.' For the first time Jack Pusey looked and sounded self-conscious. 'How long will you be staying this time?'

'I'm not sure.' Fiona smiled at him, and Phyllida hoped she had managed to make the smile unprovocative. 'I'm not trying to be mysterious,' she said. 'I really haven't decided.'

'No job to go back to?' Jack asked her, then immediately apologised for his nosiness.

'It's all right.' Phyllida liked his diffidence, and he had given her—had given Fiona, she corrected herself—an opening. 'I don't have a job just now, but I'll ask you what yours is.'

'I'm director of Seaminster's cute little Botanic Gardens. I don't suppose you've been—'

'Yes I have. Jack! They're lovely.'

'I think so.'

'You're a botanist, then?'

'That's it.'

'I used to be an actress. Very obscurely.'

'You surprise me, somehow,' he said, looking at her.

It was a professional compliment, but Phyllida was not in a mood to savour it. 'Long ago and far away,' she said dismissively, looking at her watch. 'I'm afraid I must go, I'm expecting a phone call' In a way she wanted to go, there was so little she could say.

He got to his feet without protest. 'By car or on foot?'

'On foot, I think, it's fine and it's such a short way.'

They walked in silence, and Phyllida wondered if she had ever felt so sad.

'May I ring you?' he asked on the hotel steps.

'I don't think your wife would like that either, Jack.' If there was a wife, it would make it so much easier.

'There is no wife, Fiona. Not now.'

'I'm afraid there's a husband, though,' Fiona said gently. It helped a bit to remind herself that it wasn't Phyllida Moon Jack Pusey wanted to see again. And she might be able to make it help that he was the only man in the art class with whom she could imagine Carol Hargreaves having had an affair.

'Ah. I thought there might be.' He gave her a friendly grin. 'I'll see you at the class next week, Fiona. Goodnight.'

'Goodnight, Jack.'

Looking up as usual at the Agency windows when he had walked away, Phyllida was glad for the first time that they were dark.

Chapter Twelve

Kendrick's office desk had its back to the window, but it was a long time since he had swivelled his large leather chair in order to look out. He had found himself alone for the few moments preceding the arrival of Dr Piper and Miss Bowden, and his eyes were on Great Hill, balefully bright and detailed under a kinetic sky, before he had realized what he was going to do.

'Thank you, Miriam,' he murmured, according her his pleasure in the unaccustomed sensation of rest that the long view gave his eyes. As he gazed he decided it would be commonsense to intersperse his daylong close views—of faces alive and dead, baggage significant and pathetic, microscopic evidence, the piece of stairway in front of him he needed to see so as not to fall up or down, the TV when he got home—with longer ones. And he lived by the sea, for God's sake, which offered the best long views in the world, a fact he had once upon a time appreciated . . .

Oh Miriam!

All that had happened was that she had brought Jenny for her regular visit and hadn't handed her over at the front door in the usual way, she had come in with her and stayed till it was time to take her home. She had joined them on the sands and they had sat side by side against a rock watching Jenny run about with a couple of other children and some dogs. One of the dogs had been Miriam's dog, Sam, whom this time Miriam had released from his special compartment at the back of her car. It was the first time Kendrick had seen more of his wife's dog than a profile through a car window. The dog had turned out to be an agreeable creature, a rough-haired, medium-sized brown mongrel with a cheerful and

136

philosophical disposition who had been happy to respond to Kendrick's overtures and had deposited a large turd on his back lawn. When the day was over Kendrick had gone out into the mild spring evening to deal with the turd and had found himself absurdly reluctant to remove it, evidence as it was of Miriam's presence in his house. Eventually he had taken it on a shovel to the very bottom of the garden and buried it in a patch of unused soil.

He still knew Miriam well enough to feel confident she too had enjoyed the day. He had had nothing to lose, and hadn't found it hard at any point to be relaxed, not to press her, not to ask for anything more than she had been miraculously prepared to give him. She had been a little wary, a bit on the defensive, at the beginning, but that had been the least of his fears, and by lunchtime she had seemed to be as relaxed as he was and several times she had laughed without restraint. The wonderful clear, sudden laugh he had loved and had never thought to hear again.

Even when she left he had managed not to say anything to alarm her, although his murmured 'It would be nice if you felt like doing this again,' as they said goodbye would have had her shying away from him in horror in the early days of their separation. This time she had said 'Maybe I will,' and smiled into his eyes.

So it had been the best day he had lived through for more than two years, marred only by the tremulously hopeful look Jenny had turned on them both just before getting into the car and his mental picture of how she would look if her mother told her it had only been a one-off . . .

As he reluctantly swivelled back to his desk, Kendrick wondered why he had made such heavy weather of Miss Bowden, and why he had felt so grudging of her undoubted assistance. Then laughed aloud himself as he wondered if it was anything to do with his disappointment at being denied the compensation of Mrs Sunbury.

Miss Pym was so totally uncharismatic he did have to shake off a touch of the old irritation as she appeared a step or two behind Dr Piper, but he managed to include her in his welcome. It was only when he saw one of Piper's eyebrows go up and Miss Pym's narrow eyes widen—was there a flash of violet?—that he realized his invariably cool manner towards them had acquired a touch of geniality, and he wanted to laugh again.

'When you said you had things to tell me I decided it was time for another meeting,' he said, as the door clicked behind the PC who had followed them in with the coffee tray. 'Anything from last night at Trenchard's?' he asked Peter.

'Only that my visit left me wondering what's to become of them. Hargreaves looks as though he's wasting away, and Trenchard was hardly more than a zombie. The honours were done by Trenchard's brother Daniel. At least he seems a tower of strength, placid and laid back. He told me privately that Trenchard can't stop imagining what killed his wife: watching the death of her friend, being manhandled, not being able to find her friend and then coming across her before the murderer had left the scene. It was a pretty depressing evening.' Peter paused. 'Miss Bowden has one or two things to tell you, Chief Superintendent.'

Kendrick detected a wary edge to Dr Piper's announcement. 'I'm listening.'

'Miss Pym went to the library yesterday morning,' Phyllida said, 'and sat reading where she'd sat when Sally was on duty.' She heard Peter's catch of breath, and realized she had forgotten to tell him that despite his injunction to rest she had spent the whole of the preceding day in his employ. 'I intended staying for perhaps an hour, listening for any staff or public reactions, but I'd only been there a few minutes when Jeremy Clark was leaning over me and inviting Miss Pym for a coffee in the café while he told her his worries about Sally. He'd apparently felt the way I've felt—and I think you have as well, Chief Superintendent, from what you've told us—that Sally was withholding some knowledgesfre has about the disappearance and deaths of her mother and Maggie Trenchard. He suggested she might be less on her guard with Miss Pym, and wondered if she might be able to find out something she could pass on to him. Miss Pym agreed to try of course, but if she succeeds she obviously won't be telling Jeremy Clark.'

'No. She'll be telling Dr Piper, and Dr Piper will be telling me. Do you feel there's still a chance Sally may unburden to her?'

'When Miss Pym had ascertained that Jeremy Clark's flat has a guest bedroom with bathroom en-suite she told Sally she was looking for a respectable, cheap guest-house for the summer, and Sally invited her to stay at the flat while she made enquiries for her. Sally rather jumped at the chance, in fact, because Jeremy Clark is about to go away on a job.'

Kendrick's face showed no reaction, but when he spoke, after a pause to gaze at her, Phyllida thought she could see admiration in his eyes. 'Well done, Miss Bowden. I take it Miss Pym accepted?'

'Yes. With the mental reservation that she would tell Sally she'd found guest-house accommodation for herself if you objected. Dr Piper was going to tell you on the telephone, but when you invited us—'

'I don't object,' Kendrick interrupted. Perhaps he should. It was so long since he had been professionally uncertain of what he was doing it felt like the first time. But this was new territory for him, territory he had never thought to tread so near the top of his professional tree. 'So long as you keep Miss Pym in place if there is the slightest chance of anyone seeing you.'

'Of course. Sally's invited her to Sunday lunch at the Trenchard house, which could be useful. If there's anything to learn.'

'It's always useful to observe reactions. I'm grateful'Kendrick said it quite easily.

'Thank you. Now, Miss Cummings. Mrs Steele saw her in the window of Robinson's Café before the art class and joined her for a snack. Even now it's known that Mrs Hargreaves and Mrs Trenchard were murdered she's still talking the way she apparently talked to her fellow student in the ladies' loo. She presents her disapproval of the dead women as moral rectitude, but I suspect a lot of it's plain jealousy and sexual frustration. Her views on just about everyone in the class were highly cynical, but although she implied that Mrs Hargreaves had got what she asked for, she didn't actually go so far as to accuse anyone.

'During the break, Jack Pusey invited Mrs Steele for a post-class drink, and when they went back for the second half, Miss Cummings heard him tell Mrs Steele he'd see her later. I caught her glaring at Mrs Steele several times during the second half of the class, and Jack told me over the drinks that he'd been a bit more civil to her than any of the other students ever were, though not to the extent of accepting her invitation to a concert. So I suspect that whatever she told me—and it didn't really amount to anything—was coloured by her frustrations. Mrs Steele had a few words with almost everyone, which only reinforced my impression that they're pretty normal—with the exception perhaps of a very edgy chap whom nobody likes. Albert Paterson, it's in here.' Phyllida pushed her notes across the desk. 'I'm sorry it doesn't say very much.'

'You've done very well,' Kendrick told her, because with his irritation out of the way he saw that he believed it. And that Miss Bowden's work could carry a peculiar cost. 'I suppose,' he said to her, with a tentativeness that felt as unfamiliar as his new sense of doubt, 'that the way you work, sometimes you must feel uncomfortable, perhaps regretful when one of your characters has to disappear after forming some kind of a relationship?' He was feeling a bit uncomfortable himself to discover how hard it had become to empathise. 'I was thinking of this Mr Pusey, who invited Mrs Steele for a drink. He could be—hurt, perhaps, when she disappears without a word? Your characters *do* disappear without a word, I hope, Miss Bowden?' Kendrick added sharply, suddenly and strictly professional.

'Oh, yes, Chief Superintendent. Always. And you're quite right, I can feel both uncomfortable and regretful.' Phyllida had already decided, with Peter's reluctant agreement, that Miss Pym vis-à-vis Sally would be an exception to her rule (if only by post), but neither she nor Peter had any intention of revealing that to Kendrick.

'How long are you thinking of staying with Miss Hargreaves?' Kendrick asked Phyllida.

'I thought till, say, Monday afternoon. Sally'll be at the library on Monday morning, when I can have a look round and see if I can find anything on paper about any knowledge she may have about her mother's death. Though I'm hoping she might have told me before then, if there is anything.'

'I think it would be an idea to extend that by twenty-four hours if you feel you can,' Kendrick said. 'Because the funeral has been arranged for Monday morning. Hargreaves and Trenchard didn't hold out on you last night, Dr Piper, they only learned this morning that this was the first time available, and they took it. It has to mean Sally Hargreaves having a day off work, and being around the flat when she isn't in church and wherever the mourners go afterwards. So I think Miss Pym should arrange her departure for Tuesday afternoon, giving her the clear stretch of Tuesday morning.' Kendrick made a further effort in the direction of empathy. 'And it could seem a bit out of character for Miss Pym to announce that she's leaving on the day of all days when Miss Hargreaves will be glad of a bedtime shoulder.'

'We appreciate that,' Peter and Phyllida said in unison, and the three of them laughed together for the first time.

It enabled Kendrick to say that there had been no further developments so far as the police were concerned. When he had said it he waited for the anger to swell inside him, but it didn't come, there was only the professional frustration which once upon a time had been his sole reaction to stalemate or setback. *Miriam, please stay near.*

'Alibis are pretty useless in a situation where Forensics are unable to give a time of death more precise than within thirty-six hours.' The roundabout was back before his mind's eye, but the fear of defeat that accompanied it was remaining manageable and he was going to be able to keep it out of his voice. 'Granted it's more than likely the women died on the day they disappeared, all we know is that it has to be after, say, twelve noon. Wilkins and Jones can't give us satisfactory alibis after one-thirty to two pm, but the women could have been dead by then. Or they could have been alive still the next day.'

Kendrick was astonished to find himself thinking aloud to laymen on professional matters and seeing it as something potentially helpful rather than a shameful example of *lèse-majesté*. 'Sally Hargreaves had the afternoon off work the day her mother and Mrs Trenchard disappeared, and had arranged to meet them in the Marigold Café for tea at half-past-three, but they didn't show up, so at least we can pinpoint the time of their disappearance if not the time of their deaths. We've been all over Mr Wilkins'.car and his and Jones's homes, and there was nothing. Easier, though, not to leave traces when you strangle. No weapons, no blood. No scarf or stocking, in this instance. Carol Hargreaves was killed with a pair of hands. Thank you both for coming in.'

Peter and Phyllida got to their feet, for the first time beating Kendrick to it. 'Miss Bowden probably won't feel able to leave Miss Hargreaves' flat over the weekend,' Peter said. 'But she'll keep in touch with me via her mobile phone. And I'll keep in touch with you.'

'Thank you.' Kendrick realised, without, the dismay he would once have experienced, that he had forged an alliance which was likely-to last.

'You don't have to be quite so independent,' Sally chided Miss Pym gently, as she helped the old lady out of her taxi. 'I'd have been so very pleased to collect both you and your belongings.' Merely watching for her house guest out of her bedroom window had been an occupation Sally had welcomed, she was so tired of drifting round the flat picking things up and putting them down again. But there was so little, now, that she would ever really want to do, now that she could never ask her mother to forgive her ...

When she saw the taxi turning in at the gate she had hurtled downstairs, and was out on the forecourt, shivering in the sharp breeze, as it drew up.

'That's very kind of you, dear. But it isn't easy to cast aside habits of independence learned of necessity over a lifetime and—'

'Miss Pym!' Sally interrupted, shocked out of her apathy for another welcome moment by the sight of the meagre contents of the taxi's boot. 'This can't be *all* of your things?'

'Oh, no, dear. Not quite. I've arranged for the bulkier items to go into store. My mother's little desk and so on ... They were collected just before I left, so it has all worked out nicely. I'm very grateful to you, Sally.'

'And I'm grateful to *you*. The—the funeral's on Monday, and

Jeremy's coming back, of course, for that, but he'll be off again immediately afterwards and not home properly until Thursday. You're doing me a tremendous favour, Miss Pym.'

'It's very satisfactory,' Miss Pym observed, as she trotted beside Sally towards the building in the wake of the encumbered driver, 'when an arrangement suits all parties. It doesn't happen as often as one might suppose.'

'I hadn't thought . . . I'm paying for your taxi, Miss Pym, at least and I'm having no argument.'

Phyllida looked at Sally's suddenly resolute white face, and knew she must give in. 'Thank you, dear. I have money ready, of course, but if you really want to . . . I don't take it for granted, you know.'

'Of course I know.' Sally added a generous tip and asked for the two shabby suitcases to be carried upstairs. When the driver had deposited them in the hallway of the flat she leaned against the front door to click the latch, and Phyllida saw the flash of relief across her face which seemed to leave it even more unhappy then it had been before.

'Are the Press still troubling you, dear?' Miss Pym asked as she drew off her gloves.

'No.' Sally half wished they were, it would postpone her mother's further disappearance, into the past. 'The funeral's at half-past-eleven on Monday, so I'm taking the day off work.'

'Yes, of course. I'm afraid you'll have to be ready for the Press there, dear.'

'I shan't care who's there, and who isn't, I just want to get it over.' Her mother in a box, on her way to be burned, unable to hear what at every minute of every day she was crying out to say to her. If she could just escape from herself, not be Sally Hargreaves any more, she might bear the burden of being alive while her mother was dead.

'I can understand that, Sally. I'm sorry you've had to wait so long, but I suppose it could have been longer.'

'I suppose so.' Making a savage effort to control her thoughts, Sally picked up the suitcases. 'You can unpack as much as you want now, while I'm making tea, and then we'll relax together and look at the sea.' *Relax*! Sally almost laughed aloud. 'This isn't exactly a luxury flat,' she heard herself say as she pushed open the door of the smaller bedroom with her knee. 'But it does have two bathrooms en-suite, as you know, which I think is quite civilised. So you're quite self-contained.'

Phyllida exhaled a long, quiet breath of relief, realising that she had been braced for Sally to say she was sorry, but she was afraid she needed access to the guest bathroom because of features in it that were absent from her own ... And the bedroom door had a bolt.

'I consider a private bathroom to be the acme of luxury,' Miss Pym pronounced, carefully removing her hat and placing it on the flowered bedspread. 'It's something I am unused to these days, and I shall enjoy it. Yes, I shall just remove one or two things from my cases now, Sally, and then I'll join you for a very welcome cup of tea.'

'You look tired,' Sally said, forcing herself to be aware of something that was not taking place in her own head. 'If you want to rest any time please don't hesitate to retire in here.'

'I won't, Sally.' It had been worth emphasising the pallor. 'But I'll be with you in a moment.'

Alone, and having silently drawn the bolt, Phyllida quickly unpacked Miss Pym's other skirt and her two changes of blouse, hung them in the fitted wardrobe, and took her washing things into the small internal bathroom. The immediate gentle roar of the fan when she switched on the light would muffle her voice on the mobile, and there was another bolt. So she would be doubly protected while she carried out the facial transformation which must take place each morning. Miss Pym would have to disappear at night in the interests of both the bed linen and Phyllida's skin.

It was Sally who voiced Phyllida's remaining fear. 'In the morning,' she said, as they settled back in their chairs with mugs and biscuits and looked involuntarily towards the vast view, 'you just stay in bed until I bring you a cup of tea. There'll be no rush,' Sally added drearily.

'That's very kind of you, dear, and I hope you won't think me ungrateful if I say that, although I appreciate it, I would rather see you when I'm up and dressed. I know I'm old-fashioned but once upon a time—oh, dear, this sounds ridiculous now but I'm talking about another world—it was only the maids and one's mother who saw one in *déshabillé*, and I still feel awkward about it. So if you'll just give a tap on the door when you want me to get up, I'll have my tea with you when I'm dressed and ready.'

'Of course.' Somewhere the far side of her nightmare Sally found Miss Pym's modesty endearingly eccentric, especially as she had surprisingly good teeth and couldn't be afraid of being seen without them. 'That's fine. I'll give you a knock when I'm getting up myself. I always ask for one when I'm staying with friends, because if you're told to sleep as long as you want you spend half the night waking in case you abuse your host's generosity and sleep till lunchtime.' Yes, she had once worried about things like that.

'That's so true, dear!' Miss Pym responded. 'What a lovely view this is!'

Gazing with love over her adored seascape, Phyllida felt an absurd pang of homesickness for her bright little house at the other end of the bay, focusing her mind's eye on the shadow of the stained-glass blue-tit, the centre of the panel in her front door, which the sunlight elongated down the pale wall above the telephone in the hall. By now the sun would be low enough to have made the bird climb to the point where the tip of the twig on which it was perched began to bend as it reached the frame of the looking-glass above it . . .

'Would you like to play cards, Miss Pym? Canasta? Bezique?'

Miss Pym opted for bezique, which she had loved as a girl, and they had a couple of games, winning one each. Then some sherry. They were drinking it when the telephone rang, and Phyllida heard half a conversation with Jeremy Clark which brought some life back into the girl's face.

'You really care for him, don't you?' Miss Pym said, as Sally switched off.

'Oh, yes. If I didn't have Jeremy . . .'

'How did you meet, Sally?'

The story of a spilled ice-cream at Seaminster Playhouse took them to the point where the casserole was ready. It was good, and Miss Pym chided Sally for moving her portion about her plate rather than eating it. 'You have to keep your strength up, and this is just the sort of nourishing food to help you do so.'

'At the moment it could choke me. I'll make myself drink a glass of milk before I go to bed.'

'That's right, dear. And I think that should be early, for both of us.' Looking at Sally's blank face, Phyllida knew there would be no revelations that night, and halfway through the TV news she yawned and sighed. Sally asked her if she had had enough.

'It's all very interesting,' Miss Pym said, 'but I'm afraid I'm having a little difficulty staying awake.'

'I wish I was. But I've had enough, too.' Sally switched the set off. 'Shall we go to bed?'

It was just eight o'clock. Under the blankets which formed the main contents of Phyllida's two suitcases there were several paperback books of escapist fiction. In bed at nine after a long, deep bath, with a view of her own face in the mirror at the foot of the bed, Phyllida smiled at her reflection and settled down to read. There was nothing else she could do, and she found to her amusement that her first round-the-clock employment felt like a holiday. But she had had a long journey to get there, and within a few minutes the book had slipped from her hand and she was asleep.

Across Seaminster, Chief Superintendent Kendrick also slept early. He had eaten his supper in his armchair, the tray on the small table that just fitted over his high knees, savouring with a mixture of happiness and apprehension the prospect of seeing Miriam in the morning. While he played with his steak he watched the news, then, too tired to move, left the television on in the hope that it would act like a lullaby. It obliged: almost as soon as he had pushed the table away he was hovering above a traffic island topped by a cypress tree, which as he slowly descended he saw was Anita Sunbury, immensely tall and disturbingly female in black leather. She was lashing the bare backs of a cowering Wilkins and Jones with a long flexible whip, while Miss Pym signalled apologetically from the shelter of a tree—even in his dream Kendrick was aware of his sense of triumph at having proved Miss Pym and Mrs Sunbury to be two different people. But then Miss Pym's face was distorted by terror and he saw that a disembodied arm had appeared from behind the tree and was locked round her throat. But it was no longer Miss Pym who was being drawn backwards out of his sight, it was a woman he had never met but whose photograph he had learned by heart. Carol Hargreaves.

He had landed on the roundabout, but his legs refused to take him behind the tree where Carol Hargreaves had been dragged. All he could do was lean painfully forward, just far enough to see her struggling and gasping, and the hands round her throat. Large hands, a man's hands . . . If he could manage just one step, he was so very near . . . But the pain of trying to move was so excruciating it woke him up, and it took several minutes for the arm he had been lying against to come fully back to life, and the stinging of the pins and needles to subside. And to accept that he still had no idea whatsoever who had strangled Carol Hargreaves, and encouraged Maggie Trenchard to die.

'I'm looking forward to seeing the little boy,' Miss Pym said to Sally in the car the next morning.

'Ross is fifteen. But he's like a little boy, yes. And a welcome distraction at the moment on a Sunday, he needs so much attention. But I've a feeling that now Maggie isn't there, Frank will stop bringing him out, especially if Daniel—that's his brother—isn't free to join us. Daniel's so good with Ross and he likes doing things for him.'

'Is Daniel coming today?'

'Daddy said not, so maybe Ross won't be there either. Luckily Ross won't miss it. He likes some people more than others, but he's happy with anyone who's kind to him. Maggie was wonderful with him.'

Phyllida suspected a sob. 'Will you be going to Mr Trenchard's every Sunday, never to your own home?'

Sally shuddered. 'I haven't been home since—since Mummy wasn't there. That's dreadful, I know, and I'll have to force myself soon or I'll never go again; Daddy's putting the house on the market. Anyway, Frank insists on our going to him because of Ross making a mess when he eats, and as Frank's a bit dicey at the moment we'd go along with him anyway.'

A bit dicey. This was corroboration of what Peter had reported about Frank Trenchard, and Phyllida began to wonder how he would react to the extra guest. 'I presume your father and Mr Trenchard are aware that I'm coming?' Miss Pym asked.

'Yes, I told them. Well, I asked Frank if it was all right, to be honest,' Sally added reluctantly. As I said, his reactions are a bit-unpredictable at the moment.'

'And what was his reaction, Sally?'

'He just . . . he just *growled*.' Sally forced herself to laugh. 'Then Daddy said he was glad you were coming with me, and Frank sort of subsided. Daddy's pleased you're staying with me, especially while Jeremy's away. If I was alone he'd probably come to me each night for his evening meal, but we're . . . well, we're neither of us very comfortable with one another at the moment.'

'I think I can understand that, dear.' For weeks after her mother had died, Phyllida and her father had been unable to meet each other's eyes.

Matthew Hargreaves let them in. Phyllida thought she saw shock in the eyes of both father and daughter at the impact of their mutual disarray, and then they were in each other's arms for a brief hug before Matthew turned with a courteous smile to Miss Pym and Sally introduced them. As he led the way into the sitting-room Sally whispered, 'Silence. No Ross,' and Phyllida heard her sigh. Wearing the old lady like a coat of mail—she managed an inward smile at the incongruous conceit—Phyllida stood self-deprecatingly at the sitting-room door, advancing only when Sally urged her forward.

'This is Miss Pym, Frank. We're friends from the library, as I told you, and she's a great comfort in the flat while Jeremy's away,'

'Hm.' Frank Trenchard was sitting slumped in an armchair as

Peter had described him, his head on his chest, the glass with the amber liquid on the table beside him. But when he slowly looked up at her, Phyllida was aware of the clarity of his gaze and her instinct told her that, as yet at least, he was no alcoholic. For a fanciful moment she imagined him transferring his decline to Matthew Hargreaves, who looked so pale and gaunt his eyes dominated his face like the eyes of a mortally sick man.

'You're very welcome, Miss Pym,' Matthew Hargreaves said quietly, looking anxiously at Frank Trenchard. 'It's good for Sally to have a companion while Jeremy's away,' he said, raising his voice.

'Hm,' Frank Trenchard repeated, then motioned impatiently towards the sofa. 'You'd better sit down, madam.'

'Thank you.' Phyllida sat neatly down, and Sally said she must put the casserole in the oven and ran out of the room. 'I'm . . . so very sorry,' Miss Pym said tremulously.

Frank Trenchard grunted and Matthew Hargreaves thanked her. Miss Pym said she had hoped to meet Mr Trenchard's son.

'Daniel—Frank's brother—was unable to join us today.' Matthew Hargreaves spoke very softly, and Phyllida's second image of him was as a battery running down. 'Sally will have told you that Ross has difficulties'—Hargreaves glanced across at Trenchard, and looked relieved that he showed no reaction—'and Daniel is wonderful with him. So Frank decided—as things are just now—not to bring him home today.'

'I see. Yes. It's very kind of you to let me join you, Mr Trenchard,' Miss Pym said. Phyllida found that, like Matthew Hargreaves, she had raised her voice, but the only response was a rumble.

'It's kind of *you* to stay with Sally,' Hargreaves said. 'She's having difficulty.'

'Aren't we all!' The angry shout from Trenchard made both Phyllida and Hargreaves start.

'Of course, Frank,' Matthew Hargreaves soothed. Phyllida wondered whether it was strength of character or an inability to feel deeply which was enabling him to face up to the tragedies so much more successfully than his friend.

It was an unhappy gathering at the lunch table, sharpening Phyllida's awareness of the difference between her work for the Agency and her work on stage—the racked characters around her now could never join her own eventual escape into the wings.

Everyone seemed relieved when the meal was over. Sally took Miss Pym for a little walk round the large and beautifully tended garden. 'Maggie wasn't strong enough to garden and Frank isn't interested, so they have help and that's one thing that hasn't gone to pot,' Sally said bitterly when Miss Pym had exclaimed in delight at some spring blossom. 'Daddy and Mummy both love gardening but I suppose Daddy ...' Sally started at Miss Pym in horror. 'I don't know,' she whispered. 'I don't know if Daddy's still looking after the garden because I haven't been back to the house.'

'You'll have to go soon, Sally. For your own sake as well as his.'

'I suppose so.' Sally looked at her watch. 'It's three o'clock.' Phyllida heard the relief in her voice. 'We can go back to the flat. It's dreadful, but we've nothing to say to one another. I sometimes wish I didn't have to see them, even my father.'

'That's very sad, Sally.' And when they got home, Miss Pym would comment further.

Phyllida was all the more determined on this when she saw the wistfulness in Matthew Hargreaves' face as he said goodbye.

'I don't think you can put off going home much longer, Sally,' Miss Pym said, when they were back in the flat and she came into the sitting-room after taking off her hat and gloves. 'You're the one who should see to your mother's clothes. And you don't want your father making a shrine of her belongings.' Phyllida had had a brief but horrific struggle with her own father, which she had won while he was at work by removing everything personal of her mother's from the house and refusing to tell him where they had gone until she was sure he was sane again. The clothes and some of her mother's other belongings she had given to charity, but she had kept some things in store and brought them out only a few months ago to put in the first home she had owned.

'Oh, God, Miss Pym ...' She had got through, Sally was staring at her in horrified comprehension. 'I never thought ... I don't think

Daddy ever would do anything like that, but if I don't go and see I can't be sure.'

'Precisely, Sally.'

'Oh, I will go! I never thought . . . I just thought about myself.'

Phyllida decided she could mark up one positive achievement of her weekend.

'That's understandable. But now that you *have* thought, has your father said anything about your mother's things? What he thinks of doing with them?'

'No. But I haven't encouraged him. I haven't had any views about him putting the house on the market. Oh, God, I've been so selfish!'

'You can put everything right if you go soon. Why not go tomorrow? Instead of letting the funeral car pick you up here, drive over to your father's and leave with him from the house. There won't be time for you to stay long, but it will be a start and it will please him. And then you can go a second time more easily.'

'Yes! Oh Miss Pym, I'm so glad you're here, I think you've been sent.'

'No, Sally, I'm here because of your kindness. Now, I've been invited to have coffee tomorrow morning with a friend who's staying at the Golden Lion, so perhaps you'd be kind enough to drop me there on your way through town.'

'But it'll be too early for you, the funeral's at half-past eleven so if I'm going home I'll have to leave here round about half-past nine. I'll order you a taxi—'

'Half-past nine will suit me very well, Sally, I rather enjoy sitting in a hotel lobby, watching people come and go. And if it's a nice day I'll go for a walk.'

'Well, if you mean that of course I'll take you.' Sally picked up the telephone. 'I'll just tell Daddy.'

'And I'll go to my room.'

To tell Peter there would be time for a female mourner to call in at the Agency the next morning before they made their separate ways to the town church.

Chapter Thirteen

The town of Seaminster had been optimistically named in the thirteenth century for a cathedral that had never been built, but the parish church, its original eighteenth century structure so overlaid with nineteenth century improvements it appeared at first sight to be Victorian, was imposing enough on its green mound a short way inland from Little Hill on the west arm of the bay.

When Phyllida arrived twenty minutes before the joint funeral of Carol Hargreaves and Maggie Trenchard, most of the green had disappeared under the surge of people on foot, the double ring of parking space surrounding it was full, and the police were directing the continuing line of traffic into a conveniently adjacent field. Phyllida's taxi was in an alternative queue which was just able to thread its way between the stationary vehicles defining the mound and disgorge its passengers at the church door. Britain's most bizarre modern murder was evidently still a *cause célèbre*; had the church been in the centre of town Seaminster would have come to a standstill.

Glad to be free of the frail Miss Pym and aware of the soft spring air on her liberated face, Phyllida pushed her way through the excluded media jostling at the door, gave a spur-of-the-moment name in a low, sad voice to a black-coated sentinel in the bottleneck of the porch, and walked on with relief into the body of the church. Priority was to find herself one of the few remaining seats, and she secured a narrow berth on the edge of a rear pew before attempting to look round.

The sober elegance of the congregation in front of her was an indication that police and sentinels had managed to restrict it in the main to *bona fide* family, friends and acquaintances, and she was glad to see the back of Peter's fair head a few pews ahead of her, just behind the dark curls that topped surrounding heads by several inches and proclaimed Chief Superintendent Kendrick. The ginger head further along Kendrick's pew looked familiar, and when it turned towards CS Kendrick, Phyllida recognized the sharp features of Sandy Dixon, crime reporter on the Seaminster Globe. Peter had taught her to be wary of Sandy, but she found herself approving the parochial partiality which had made him the exception to the rule excluding the media.

Feeling more and more comfortably invisible, Phyllida settled down to look and listen as objectively as she could manage through her sense of outrage for Sally and her family, that they must be exposed to so public an ordeal. Her mother and Maggie, Sally had told her, had been 'Christmas and Easter Christians' and on the parish register, and Phyllida suspected that others in the same position were taking advantage of it to satisfy their curiosity.

He that believeth in me . . .

The procession was in the aisle, already on its way past her. The coffins were side by side, the profiles of the bearers rigid with the double strain of the weight and what they must see at that moment as the prime necessity of their lives to keep their burdens precisely abreast. Phyllida didn't recognise any of them, but following them were Matthew and Jeremy with Sally between them on an arm of each. No way of seeing their faces, nor that of Frank Trenchard immediately behind, walking better than Phyllida had expected, in a trio with a man of about his height, but thinner and with more hair, and a small, stout woman in an ugly purple hat. Daniel Trenchard was a widower, so the woman must be the sister Sally had told Miss Pym they had.

We brought nothing into this world, and it is certain we can carry nothing out.

Sally had been doubtful about the Book of Common Prayer version of the funeral service her father and Frank had insisted on, but Phyllida was glad to be reminded of its stark poetry, especially as the small, insignificant-looking vicar had a strong and beautiful voice. He used it to powerful effect, following a choir-led singing of *The Lord's my Shepherd* and the stipulated prayers, to talk about the women and 'the sin against the Holy Ghost' that had destroyed them in their prime. Phyllida, a hopeful agnostic, was unable to see the deaths in orthodox religious terms, but found herself admiring the vicar for putting them into his own context. And he went on to draw what sounded like a comprehensive sketch of each of the dead women—of Carol's strength and Maggie's pliancy—the accuracy of which Sally would assess for Miss Pym that evening.

Sally! When the coffins had disappeared towards the furnace and the family began to move into the aisle, a few people round Phyllida slipped out of the church. Phyllida could have gone with them—should have gone, she knew—but her concern for Sally kept her in her place and as they came face to face Sally's eyes met her compassionate gaze and the staring blank of Sally's flared into angry and suspicious life.

As the family disappeared Phyllida was forced out of her pew by the anxiety of the people behind her to follow the stars, and let herself be carried by the crowd through the porch and out on to the path, where she saw that the husbands, Sally and Jeremy had already formed themselves into a short receiving line.

Phyllida's hope was to sidle past on the far edge of the throng, but as she started to veer away her arm was jerked from her side so fiercely she was forced to stop, and when she looked round it was again into Sally's hostile face.

'And what can *you* tell me about my mother?' Sally shouted.

'I . . . I'm sorry, I don't.'

'For God's sake, Sally!'

Frank Trenchard had followed Sally through the crowd, and as he seized her arm Sally dropped Phyllida's and her eyes went blank. Trenchard's attention was on Sally to the welcome exclusion of Phyllida, and as he urged her gently away, his arm round her shoulder, Phyllida felt it safe to linger until she had registered that Matthew Hargreaves was talking absorbedly to the vicar and seemed unaware of what had just taken place. Jeremy too, she deduced, had failed to witness the mini-drama: he was looking inquiringly from Sally to Frank Trenchard.

Shaken as much by her brief unprofessionalism as by Sally's outburst, Phyllida set off down the mound, her mood improved by a look back over his shoulder from Chief Superintendent Kendrick when he had overtaken her. As she widened her eyes in enquiry he stared at her more keenly for an instant, then turned away with a shrug, quickening his pace.

When Peter drew up at the appointed meeting place on the promenade Phyllida was there.

'Just as well you called in at the Agency,' he greeted her as she got into the car. 'Or I'd have been had up for kerb crawling. You look wonderfully anonymous.'

'Kendrick wasn't sure for a moment. And there was something else, I'm afraid.' She told him about her encounter with Sally. 'It could have been at a cost,' she finished. 'I was out of line.'

'Sally's your weak spot, isn't she?' Peter commented. His rare criticisms were nearly always expressed as statements of fact rather than as accusations.

'It looks like it.'

It'll be on the news,' he said, as he swept into his parking space behind the Square.

'Oh, God, Peter . . .'

'Don't worry. The lady in black doesn't exist.'

'Kendrick thinks she does.'

'So we'll have to come clean with him, otherwise he'll divert his forces to finding her.'

'Yes. And I've probably made things even worse for the families.' Phyllida just managed not to use the word Sally.

'Tell me again what the girl said.'

'She said "What do *you* know about my mother?" '

'Any idea what she could have meant?'

'None. Oh, Peter, I'm so sorry.'

'Look, Phyllida, all you did was stay in your pew until the family were out of the church. Now, you'd better get rid of the lady in black and recover Miss Pym as fast as you can, then get back to the flat. It could be decided Sally should spend the rest of the day at home sedated in her darkened bedroom.'

But the flat was empty when Miss Pym let herself in, and Phyllida, still aware of a tremor in her hands, went into the kitchen and put the kettle on before going to her room to remove Miss Pym's hat and gloves.

She was sitting at the kitchen counter, sipping tea and feeling very slightly better, when the doorbell rang. Sally having forgotten her key, she told herself as Miss Pym trotted to the front door, or Jeremy his and wanting something before setting off back to London . . .

But the figure distorted by the spyhole was unfamiliar, and on the doorstep Phyllida found a tall man in blue overalls with a ginger beard, a logo sewn on a pocket, and an ID in his hand. 'Mr Jeremy Clark?' the man inquired.

'This is his flat, yes, but I'm sorry, I'm afraid he isn't in at the moment. I'm just a visitor.'

'Ah.' The man hesitated. 'I don't want to pressure you,' he said, 'but I think I should take a look at the gas installation, there's been a report of a smell of gas in this building which we have to take seriously. I haven't found anything wrong in any of the other flats so it's important for me to have a look round here. Please look at my card if you feel at all unhappy.'

'That's all right. Come in.' Phyllida didn't know what a British Gas representative's ID ought to look like (she'd make a point now of finding out, and about electricity and telephone and other IDs too), but Miss Pym could hardly deny the man entry, and if he wasn't what he seemed Phyllida Moon had surprise on her side. 'In here,' she said, leading the way to the kitchen, where she indicated the boiler before excusing herself, going to her room, and transferring her gun from the base of Miss Pym's bag to her jacket pocket. *Standard procedure*, she told herself, to stifle her feeling that she was over-reacting.

'Would you like some tea?' Miss Pym inquired when she was back in the kitchen. The man was crouched down by the boiler. 'It's only just made.'

'No thanks, love. I was given a cup downstairs. Nothing wrong here,' he pronounced, straightening up. 'Now, if you'll just show me the radiators I'll be on my way.'

'Of course.' Miss Pym hovered in the doorway of each room because of being in charge of someone else's home, and the man remarked that he preferred to be kept under observation so that if there was ever an accusation of theft he had proof of his innocence.

'That's it!' he said as he came out of Miss Pym's bathroom. 'Thank you for your cooperation.' When Miss Pym let him out he nodded at the flat opposite. 'Been in there,' he said, 'so that's the lot now. False alarm. It often happens, laymen's noses aren't reliable. Good afternoon.'

By the time Sally came listlessly through the door Phyllida's unfamiliar sense of professional shortcoming had driven the gasman's visit from her mind. Miss Pym went out to the hall to welcome her. 'Are you all right, dear? You look exhausted.'

'I am.' Sally trailed into the sitting-room and flopped down in her chair. 'But I'm so very glad it's over. Seeing Mummy and Maggie sliding out of sight . . .'

'They weren't there, Sally,' Miss Pym said. 'That was the last place they would be. Did the vicar speak about them?'

'Yes. And awfully well. The only thing was he made it terribly hard not to cry. None of us did cry. I was afraid for Frank but he was all right, although he was getting prickly towards the end of the wake. We'd kept it quiet where we were going, as I told you, but of course the Press were on our tail. But we shut the door on everyone except family and one or two close friends and no one pretended to be cheerful. It didn't help that Daniel felt ill and went home to bed.'

'But it all passed off as well as you could hope.'

'No. Because I made a scene. Oh, Miss Pym, I don't know what came over me. When we were coming out of church I saw a woman at the back of the church I didn't recognise—all in black and looking *sorry* for me, and I . . . She just made all my misery come to the surface and when Daddy and Frank and Jeremy and I were forming up outside the church to greet people . . .'

'How brave of you!' Miss Pym murmured.

'Yes it was, it was a terrible ordeal. Anyway, I looked out for this woman and when I saw her I, well, I found myself running forward and grabbing her arm and asking her what she could tell me about my mother. Wasn't it dreadful? And dreadful that for a moment I didn't know what I was doing or saying. Thank heaven Daddy and Jeremy were talking and didn't notice. The surprising thing was that it was Frank who shot forward and pulled me back in line. He was so nice and sympathetic, not at all angry, I was really grateful to him.'

'How did the woman react, Sally?'

'How would you expect? She just looked bewildered and muttered something, and then of course when I'd pulled myself together she'd gone.'

'Did Frank know who she was?'

'I don't think he noticed her, he was so concerned about me.'

Miss Pym sat down, and after a turn round the room Sally threw herself into her armchair. 'Sally,' Miss Pym inquired. 'Why did you say those particular words? "What can you tell me about my mother?" '

Sally looked at her in silence from smouldering eyes, then leapt to her feet. 'I'll tell you, Miss Pym,' she shouted. 'I'll go mad if I don't tell someone. I almost told you the other day, and then at the last moment I couldn't.'

'Jeremy ... Your father ...' Phyllida repeated reluctantly, 'shouldn't it be Jeremy or your father you talk to?'

'No!' Sally screwed her face up as if she was in physical pain. 'I can't tell *them*. I can only tell someone who isn't connected with me. You'll see why. Please may I tell you?'

'All right.' Phyllida yearned to switch on the tiny recorder in Miss Pym's big bag. 'Tell me, if it will help.'

'It will.' But Sally went to the window without saying anything more, and Phyllida was beginning to think she was retreating yet again when she began to speak in a low expressionless voice.

'Mummy and Maggie came to dinner here the night after they arrived for a week's holiday at the Fountains Hotel. The night before they died. Mummy has—had—a key to the flat which Jeremy gave her in case she ever wanted a rest or the loo or something when she was shopping in Seaminster or before the art class, he's like that ... He always gets home later than me, and I thought I was going to be late myself that day because of a staff meeting and I'd told Mummy and Maggie to let themselves in and help themselves to drinks and I'd try to be there by seven. The person who was to chair the meeting was taken ill during the afternoon, so the meeting was cancelled and I left the library at my usual five-thirty ...' Sally stopped, and flung herself back into her chair. 'So it was only about a quarter-to-six when I got to the flat,' she whispered. 'I don't know, I must have opened and closed the front door rather quietly, because when I got into the hall I heard Maggie laugh'—the ashen face concertinaed again—'in a way I'd never heard before, in a way I somehow knew she wouldn't have laughed if she'd known anyone was there. It was Maggie's laugh that made me deliberately quiet, then. I went across the hall on tiptoe and I peered round the open sitting-room door—*that door?*—Sally looked fearfully across the room—'and—and Mummy and Maggie were lying on the sofa and Maggie's blouse ... Oh, God, Miss Pym, is that enough? Do you know what I'm saying?'

'Y-yes, I think ...' Miss Pym faltered, and Sally sprang to her feet again and shouted at the ceiling.

'Mummy was the chap, Maggie the girl. I saw that for myself. Before they told me, before they told me they were lovers. That was why they told me, they knew what I'd seen. They told me they'd been—like that—for a couple of years. That before then neither of them had been aware of any lesbian leanings. As if *that* was supposed to make me feel better! How easy it must have been for them to cover it up, Miss Pym! Daddy and Frank were always so pleased when Mummy and Maggie spent time together. If they'd ever been suspicious that either of them was having an affair they'd have been *reassured* when they found it was one another they were telephoning, visiting! They could even have thought they were using each other as alibis when they were—using each other!'

Sally almost screamed the last few words, then fell back into her chair. 'It's such a relief,' she whispered. 'To have told someone.'

'You really mean you haven't told Jeremy? Or your father?'

'How could I tell my *father*? *Frank*?' Sally shuddered. 'I've tried to tell Jeremy like I tried to tell you, but I couldn't.'

'Perhaps they know, and are unable to tell *you*.'

'I'm certain they don't.' Sally hadn't hesitated. 'If they did, I'd know it.'

'But Sally, if neither your father nor Mr Trenchard, nor Jeremy, know that *you* know such a, well, such a startling thing.'

Sally laughed. 'Oh, Miss Pym, since when have men been aware of women the way women are aware of men?'

'They never have, I suspect, Sally.' Phyllida paused, still feeling winded but thinking hard. 'Now, dear, there's something you'll have to expect, I'm afraid.'

Phyllida saw the leap of fear in Sally's eyes. 'What's that?'

'The Press were outside the church, weren't they? With cameras?'

'Yes, they were all over ... Oh, God!'

'They may have filmed you. If you don't want to watch the news I can watch it, and tell you.'

'I have to watch it, know the worst.' Sally had snatched up the TV listings and was running her finger down them. 'The next news is Channel Four at seven. You haven't had anything to eat, have you?'

'I'm not really hungry, Sally, and you've eaten, you won't want to—'

'I'll make you an omelette, it'll help pass the time. And we'll have a drink.'

The funeral was heralded in the last of the national headlines. Sally's outburst was there, of course. After a series of clips had reminded viewers of the case so far, the frustrated cameraman had photographed the church and its surrounds, then the bereaved both as they went in and as they came out and took up their positions by the church door. The commentary commended their courage, and then the camera was following the daughter as she ran forward, angrily accosted a woman in black, was led back to her place by the bereaved husband who was not her father, tried visibly to pull herself together. When the camera went after the woman she was out of sight among the crowd descending the hill, although Kendrick's height marked him out and both the commentator and Sally identified him. Remembering that backward glance, Phyllida hoped he might be subconsciously prepared for her confession.

'At least they didn't record what you said, Sally.'

'But lots of people must have heard it, and other news people could have recorded it. They'll be on to me, Miss Pym, asking me what I meant, who the woman was. And I don't know, I'd never seen her before, what I did didn't have anything to do with her. And now they'll blow up the shot of her and try to trace her and she's innocent!'

And non-existent, Phyllida reminded herself, although at that moment it didn't make her feel much better.

'Miss Pym,' Sally went on, springing to her feet and moving over to the window, where she stood knocking her forehead against the glass, 'I promised my mother I'd never tell a soul about her and Maggie, and now I may have told the whole world.'

'If you've repeated to me exactly what you said, Sally, then you haven't, it was far too ambiguous for anyone to interpret unless they already knew.'

It went on like that for the rest of the evening, punctuated by telephone calls from the media. Would Miss Hargreaves care to explain? After the first two Sally asked Miss Pym to answer, after the fifth they switched the phone off, and after Sally's third glass of wine Miss Pym put the bottle back in the cupboard and suggested they go to bed.

Phyllida rang Peter the moment she was in her bathroom and told him everything, and that despite the renewed media hassle Sally was determined to stick to her decision to go back to work in the morning. 'I was afraid I'd mucked that up as well, but even if she'd decided to stay at home it doesn't matter now, she's told me what I might have found out by looking round. So Miss Pym can take herself off during the morning. She's told Sally she's going into town sometime, so if she should run into her before she reaches sanctuary at the Golden Lion it'll be okay. And Peter . . .'

'Yes?'

'Miss Pym will have to leave a note, irrespective of what Phyllida Moon wants to do. If she doesn't, if she just vanishes, it will be the last straw for Sally and a hell of an embarrassment for the Chief Superintendent.'

'Yes, I can see that. Okay. I'll leave the detail to you. Kendrick's just been on, by. the way, with a piece of news. Your Miss Cummings' brother was sent down for a short spell a few years ago for GBH.'

'Heavens. I'd sort of forgotten about the art class.'

'I hope not. I told Kendrick the identity of the woman in black and he muttered something about violet eyes. He appears to think Miss Bowden has done another good job.'

'You'll have to ring him now, and tell him about the dead women. It makes you start thinking about the suspects all over again, doesn't it? If Sally's wrong and her. father knows . . . If the Art Class Two saw something like *that* . . .' A sudden sharp thought cut through Phyllida's musings. 'Peter, will you ask Mr Kendrick for Mrs Sunbury's sake, if not Miss Pym's, to wait until noon tomorrow before getting on to Sally or either of the husbands, to give Miss Pym time to disappear? I know he'll be desperate to talk to them, but it isn't long to wait.'

'Of course I will. And, dear girl, you've done wonders. It's your last night and you can sleep easy.'

'I'm tired enough.'

But although her eyes were closing as she closed her book, Phyllida was still too agitated to sleep, too relentlessly reviewing her ideas in the light of Sally's revelation. It was a couple of hours before she slipped into a restless doze punctuated by a series of replays of the gasman's visit. At first they were distorted by no more than the vagaries of the dreaming mind, but they became more and more surreal as their menace grew. Eventually, having shut the front door on a creature that was more monster than man and retired to her bedroom, Phyllida realised with a leap of terror that she could still hear footsteps in the hall.

And that she was awake.

Sally might have gone to the kitchen for a drink, but she wouldn't be fumbling at her guest-room door, gently turning the handle again and again and then doing something scratchy to the lock.

On the reflex that had never yet been tested, Phyllida sprang out of bed, pulled on her deep-pocketed dressing-gown, put one of the metal objects by her bed into one of the pockets, picked up the other in her right hand, crept barefoot across the room to the door, slid back the bolt, and after a pause which told her keen ears there was no longer someone immediately outside, opened a cautious crack and peered out.

To see the rear silhouette of a tall figure with a black egg for a head standing in Sally's open doorway. The figure was motionless, but by the safety lights shining through Sally's thin curtains Phyllida saw that it had a cushion in its hands.

'Stop where you are!' Phyllida ordered, as she found herself behind the figure with her gun against its neck.

But the figure whirled round and in one rapid movement put the cushion against her face and pushed her towards the wall. 'I meant to do you first, you old cow,' she heard it mutter, and then she raised the gun again and fired.

There was a cry of pain as the cushion fell, and through a rain of dark drops Phyllida saw that one of the strong arms had become a broken wing and was being nursed by the other. But after its single cry the figure stood mute before Phyllida's still pointing gun, heightening her shuddery sensation that she was battling an android.

The shot had roused Sally from her pill-induced sleep, and when Phyllida yelled at her to join her, she stumbled out of bed and obeyed.

'Take the gun,' Phyllida ordered then. 'Hold it steady . . .'

Sally murmured, 'Miss Pym . . .?' but did as she was told while Phyllida took her handcuffs out of her dressing-gown pocket, snapped one half of them on a wrist slippery with blood from its injured partner and ordered the now obedient figure to walk in front of her until she could wind the connecting chain round one of the slender columns heading Sally's brass bedstead before closing the second cuff.

When she saw how uncomfortably the man was dangling, and that she had shattered his right elbow, she persuaded Sally to help heave him up so that he was lying on the bed with his uninjured arm secured above his head.

'Now,' Phyllida said, switching on the overhead light and leaning towards the balaclava, 'let's have a look at him.'

Chapter Fourteen

Sally screamed as the balaclava slid upwards, and after a glance at the sullen face it had been hiding Phyllida looked towards her in surprise.

'You know him?'

'Of course! It's Daniel! Daniel Trenchard!'

And the gasman, Phyllida decided, as she studied the face. And like his brother, although when she had looked at him so casually in church that afternoon she hadn't seen it.

'You came to kill us!' Sally yelled, backing into a corner.

'I'll speak to the police. Get them here. And an ambulance.'

'You killed my mother, you and your brother! My father had nothing to do with it!'

'Of course he didn't,' Daniel Trenchard said scornfully. 'Him? He'd never have had the guts. No, it was just Frank and me.' He turned his head to look at Phyllida. 'Where's the old lady? And who the hell are you?'

'The old lady's gone and I'm someone who's done first aid, I'll try to stop the bleeding. Can you find me something, Sally?'

Sally looked in disgust at the smears of blood on her duvet cover before raiding a drawer for a couple of Jeremy's large white handkerchiefs. The man on the bed stayed silent while Phyllida bound up his wound, but his mouth was a narrow line and twice he winced.

'The police and an ambulance will come right away when we ring 999,' Sally said, advancing slowly from her corner to clutch at Phyllida's sleeve. 'I don't know who you are either, or whose side you're on, but we will call the police, won't we? Please!'

'Come outside.'

After a moment's hesitation and a blazing glance at the man on the bed, Sally preceded Phyllida into the hall. 'We'll call the police of course, Sally,' Phyllida said, the moment they were out of their prisoner's earshot. 'I work for them. But I want to call my boss first and get him to contact Chief Superintendent Kendrick. I'm here with his approval.'

'Where's Miss Pym?' Sally demanded hysterically.

'I *am* Miss Pym. I'm an actress and I sleuth in character. In twenty minutes I'll prove it to you. That's why I want to ring my boss before we contact the police, I need time to become Miss Pym again before they arrive, and he'll see I get it. If you like, you can come with me and listen in. He'll be all right. He can't get free and he won't bleed to death.'

Phyllida looked round Sally's bedroom door. Daniel Trenchard was lying motionless with his eyes closed, his face so bloodless it would have been shocking to see the seep of scarlet through the makeshift sling if all her shock had not gone already into what he had come to do. Phyllida went back to Sally, shivering in the cold of her naked self, stripped of protective disguise. Yet, even now, that self wasn't speaking or acting on its own behalf, it was still playing a part for which Phyllida Moon had learned the lines and the moves.

She led the way to the guest bedroom and, with Sally standing dazed in front of her, sat down in her usual place on the lavatory lid to ring Peter. 'Give me half an hour to revive Miss Pym,' she finished, 'then contact Kendrick. This is something he won't mind getting out of bed for. Trenchard's injury isn't life-threatening, but better ask him to arrange for an ambulance, I suppose. My name's Phyllida Moon,' she told Sally as she switched off. It was the first time she had spoken her name in the context of her work as a private eye, and it was a moment she had dreaded so profoundly she had hoped it would never come. But saying it to Sally, surprisingly, felt all right, even had a sense of relief to it. 'You're privileged,' she went on severely. 'I work anonymously because I work in character, and you're the only person I've met through my job who's seen me as I am.' By the time he came out of prison Daniel Trenchard would have forgotten what she looked like. 'So you must keep my secret, Sally. Now, I have to turn back into Miss Pym before the police arrive, even they have never seen or heard of Phyllida Moon.' Phyllida hesitated as she got to her feet. 'Will you do something for me, for both of us? Station yourself in the hall and look into your bedroom now and then to make sure he hasn't found a way of escape I didn't think of? I shan't be long, and neither will the police.'

Peter arrived just as Miss Pym was ready, and Chief Superintendent Kendrick, Detective Sergeant Wetherhead, a WPC and a couple of male uniforms ten minutes later. Five minutes after that an ambulance arrived, and the uniforms released the still silent prisoner and escorted him away in it. When he had heard a fuller version from Phyllida of what Dr Piper had told him, Kendrick rang headquarters and asked them to pick up Frank Trenchard. 'He could be awaiting a signal he's not going to receive, which he may take as a signal to leave home. Cover the back before you ring the front door bell, and if it isn't answered break the door down. I don't think we need call on Matthew Hargreaves until the morning. It doesn't appear he's involved. You won't want to stay here tonight,' he said to Sally as he put the phone down. 'With or without a companion. Where would you like us to take you?'

Sally looked instinctively towards Miss Pym, and Phyllida's hesitation was brief. 'May I take Miss Hargreaves home with me, Chief Superintendent? There's hardly enough of the night left for her to go to her father.'

'If you don't live too far away,' Kendrick said, avidly awaiting his first clue.

'I live within the boundaries of Seaminster. Is that all right?'

Kendrick stifled a sigh. 'It is, Miss Bowden.' Phyllida saw Sally's start of surprise. She would have to explain Miss Bowden too. 'And I suggest you get on your way as soon as you've got some things together. Miss Pym looked after you well, Miss Hargreaves,' he said to Sally, after an internal tussle not to.

He thought it was his second Sunday with Miriam which enabled him to be amused by the strength of the curiosity with which he awaited Miss Hargreaves' response, and his resigned disappointment when she merely agreed with him, as if it was the most natural thing in the world for a frail old lady to bring down a would-be assassin. Sally Hargreaves had clearly penetrated the mystery from which he remained excluded.

When Dr Piper and the women left, Kendrick had another struggle with himself, which this time he won, not to go to the window to see which way the car turned out of the gates.

'Kendrick's desperate to pin you down,' Peter said as he reached the promenade and drove along beside the dark void of the sea. 'D'you think he'll have put a tail on us?'

Eventually Phyllida apologized to Sally for her hysterical laughter.

'I've been away for a night or two, as you know,' she said, when Peter had gone and she was standing with Sally in her own hall, silently resuming her relationship with her house. 'So electric blankets on. Then straight to bed.'

When she had shed Miss Pym for the last time and was in her dressing-gown, Phyllida tapped on the guest room door.

Sally called to her to come in. She was already lying back in bed, and looked at Phyllida with languid approval.

'I've seen you in the library,' she said.

'I work in the reference library when I have time, I'm writing a book on women and the theatre.' Suddenly the thought of secrets made her feel sick. 'And I use your lending library too.'

'You're young,' Sally said judicially, studying Phyllida's face.

'Still young,' Phyllida corrected. 'Which isn't quite the same thing.

'I liked Miss Pym,' Sally said. 'I thought she was really sweet. But she doesn't exist. I don't feel there's anyone or anything that does.'

'Jeremy does. Don't you want to ring him?'

'Yes, but it's four o'clock. I'll ring him first thing tomorrow.'

'Before the Chief Superintendent holds his happy press conference and he could hear the news from another source.' Phyllida thought of Sandy Dixon's inquiring profile.

'I will . . . all those glimpses of Miss Pym's background, and her old-fashioned commonsense. You're a playwright as well as an actress, aren't you?'

'I suppose I am.' Phyllida hadn't thought of it.

'Are you really called Phyllida Moon?'

'I think so. Writing and acting my own scripts makes me wonder sometimes who I really am.' It was a relief to put it into words.

'That's not good,' Sally decreed.

'No. Sally ... there are a few more things I shall have to tell you, and things I hope you'll tell me. But not tonight.'

Sally struggled upright. 'Now you've said that it has to be tonight, or I shan't sleep. Things you hope *I'll* tell *you*?'

'All right. Even now I feel your unhappiness is more than grief.'

'Yes, it's guilt as well. Oh, I wanted to tell you that too, Miss ... Phyllida.'

'Can you tell me now? Will it help?'

'I don't think anything will help, but I will tell you. The night I found Mummy and Maggie—together—in the flat, I told Mummy I wanted to show her some clothes I'd bought. Maggie was lying down and Jeremy had turned on the news. Mummy was anxious to see me on my own, of course, and came with me into the bedroom. Listen ...' Sally leaned forward, her eyes begging for the comfort she knew no one could give her. 'When I'd closed the door I told her I never wanted to see her again. That I found her disgusting, and that from then on I would never think of her as my mother. I was the one who was disgusting, I was so cruel, but Mummy didn't fight back. She just looked sad—I'll never forget her face—and said she'd be in the Marigold Café the next afternoon at half-past-three on her own, and that she hoped I'd come. I told her she could please herself, but she wouldn't find me there.' Sally was now struggling openly with tears. 'But I went, of course, and by the time I got there I was desperate to take back what I'd said. To tell her I could never stop loving her ... When she didn't come it was terrible, and then when I learned why ... My mother died believing I hated her. I'll never be able to live with that, Miss Pym, Phyllida. Never, never, never!'

'Oh, Sally.' Phyllida was glad to see the storm of weeping, even though she was afraid Sally might be right. 'But when you learned she was dead, you also learned that you hadn't driven her away. You were afraid of that, weren't you?'

'Yes. She'd have come to the café, wouldn't she?' Sally asked anxiously, like a little girl. 'She'd have come if she could?'

'Of course she would.'

'Yes. Oh, God . . .'

'How did you manage not to tell Jeremy anything?' Phyllida asked, when the storm had abated.

Sally blew her nose. 'I suppose it was because Mummy disappeared so soon after I found out about her and Maggie and it was easy to hide one shock behind the other. And the guilt . . . I suppose I didn't want Jeremy to hate me for it as much as I hated—hate—myself.'

'Sally, you mustn't—'

'There's one thing I'd give anything to find out but I never will. I want to know who that woman in the church was. Mummy swore to me Maggie was the only women she'd ever . . . But the way that woman looked at me . . . Everyone looked sorry for me, of course, but that woman, it was as if she knew me. I'm going to spend the rest of my life wondering.'

'Oh, my God, Sally, I'm sorry.' The woman in black was the one secret Phyllida had hoped to keep, but Sally must be saved from a further obsession. 'The woman was another nobody, Sally. She was me.'

'Don't feed me lies!' Sally flashed. 'Not about my mother. Oh, I thought that *you*, at least . . .'

'I'm not. I'm telling you the truth. You can ask the Chief Superintendent. I came to your mother's funeral in the course of my job, to see if I could pick up any clues about her murder. I was unprofessional for a moment, I let you see how sad for you Phyllida Moon was. Which could have killed us both. I was responsible for everything that happened tonight, and I didn't want you to know.'

'But you weren't. I was the one who made the scene that made Frank . . .' Sally stiffened in horror. 'Frank knew, didn't he? That was why he understood what I shouted.'

'And for some reason he didn't want anyone else to know. Well, you and I will know the truth soon enough. And which brother is a murderer.'

The next afternoon Chief Superintendent Kendrick invited both Dr Piper and Miss Bowden to police headquarters to hear a tape of his interview that morning with Daniel Trenchard, and as a gesture of appreciation, Miss Bowden appeared as Mrs Sunbury. Both Phyllida and Peter wondered on an inward smile if that was why Kendrick told them he would sit in with them while he listened. Kendrick wondered, too.

And he had wondered during what remained of the night which brother would offer the better value, then learned in the morning that there was no choice: Frank Trenchard had lost both his sense of reality and his power of speech. But Daniel had recovered his tongue, and been ready to speak on behalf of them both.

So after the deep voice of the Chief Superintendent asking him to tell him and Detective Sergeant Wetherhead what had happened the day Carol Hargreaves and Maggie Trenchard disappeared, and a couple of lines of dialogue, Daniel Trenchard's long confession had been mostly unprompted.

'Frank came to me when he discovered his wife's secret.' The voice was dry, detached. A good voice, Kendrick had thought, for a confession.

'How did he discover it?'

'Because he knew her, of course. Because the change in her response to him told him something had happened. So he put a tail on her, and the tail delivered. Then had a fatal accident. Frank was almost insane with rage, most of all against Carol Hargreaves, who he was convinced had led Maggie astray. He was certain neither Matthew Hargreaves nor his daughter had any idea of the situation, but knowing Matthew, my brother knew that if he told him he couldn't expect him to share his fury, his need to avenge himself. But I was there, the younger brother who had always looked up to him and admired him.' There was the sound of a chair scraping on a bare floor, and Kendrick mimed his responsibility.

'Maggie had told Frank she and Carol were going into the country that Wednesday mid-morning, and we parked discreetly near the hotel I work for Frank, and I was supposed to be collecting some spares, while he was test-driving a new car. He'd driven it, in fact, straight in to my garage, which was open and waiting, and we went to the hotel in my car.

'Maggie's car was parked in the enclave in front of the hotel, and we watched them get in and drive off, then followed them. If they'd spotted us we'd have pleaded coincidence, or a surprise we were planning, but I'm a good driver and I never really thought I'd muck it up. When they turned into the track to Coombe Woods we knew where they were intending to end up so we could lag a long way behind.

'We got out of my car with theirs still out of sight, and went on on foot. When we saw their car among the trees it was empty, and then we saw them walking towards a clearing ahead.

'Even though he'd told me to put a spade in the boot I don't think Frank had any precise plans for what he was going to do—perhaps he even had a faint hope that his tail had got it wrong—but as they reached the clearing, Maggie and Carol turned to one another and started kissing. Like—*kissing*. Frank saw red then. He gave a sort of a roar and ran forwards and grabbed Carol by the throat. Maggie was clawing at his back and I ran up too and took hold of Maggie and pulled her off him. She struggled like mad for a few minutes then went limp, and . . . I don't know which of them died first. When I realised Maggie'd given out I looked up and Carol was on her back on the ground and Frank was just getting up and Carol wasn't moving. Frank said, "That's better", as if he'd just had sex or something.' Again the chair legs scraped the floor, and when Phyllida glanced towards the Chief Superintendent his face was so seriously angry she had to look away.

'I don't know what he'd intended for Maggie. I don't think he'd thought of that, he was so set on her seducer, but when he saw she was dead I think he would have flipped then and there if I hadn't reminded him we had things to do. He'd have made her pay but he wouldn't have killed her. He loved her, you see.'

'And I guess you never loved anybody, honey,' Mrs Sunbury murmured into the pause. She was the only character whose voice Phyllida retained at all times. 'You're more frightening than your brother.'

Kendrick nodded.

'We walked round the clearing looking for the best spot to bury them, and then we saw the notice.'

'What notice?' DS Wetherhead asked, into another pause.

'A notice on a pole saying "Woodland Awareness Week for Children", and then some dates starting a few days later. I almost flipped as well, then, but I said at least to get them pronto into the boot of my car and be off. Frank took Maggie's keys and drove her car to Seaminster station. We didn't want to leave it where it was and draw attention to anything the forensic people might discover, and until Maggie and Carol were found it would look as though they'd chosen to disappear. I picked him up at the station and we drove to my house. We relaxed a bit then and I remembered the gardening chap I talk to sometimes in my local who works on that roundabout. He's proud of how little work he has to do because of the tree planting, and he's told the bar more than once that it's a real wood with a space of bare earth in the middle where they only ever go when they're doing something with the central trees. So we decided to leave the bodies in the boot until three o'clock the next morning, then take them to the roundabout. It was a risk but there were two huge bonuses: by the time they were found it would be impossible to tell exactly when they'd died. And the edge of the roundabout was the end of any clues.' With the third scrape of chair legs, Kendrick met Mrs Sunbury's violet eyes and smiled ruefully.

'After we'd done a lot more talking, Frank drove the Jag back to work. He was angry, too, about the men in the art class making up to his wife, and he scribbled the note you found and left it with me. I rang in to Reception to say I'd been taken queer and hoped to be in the next day, then went off to the leisure complex. It's a long way from the garage, so there wasn't much risk in the middle of a working day. It was lunch hour and there was no class in the computer room, only a lot of idle people trying the things out, just the conditions I'd hoped for, so I typed the message and printed it out on the piece of paper I'd brought with me—a full sheet, which I held by the edges and then cut smaller when I got home. I locked myself in the garage and put the paper into the pocket in Carol's blouse and got the bodies into sacks.

'We were lucky again later. There were no motorists round the roundabout when we got there, and we didn't hear any traffic while we were on it. It was poor soil, of course, but that didn't matter, there would have been no point in burying deep. We hadn't reckoned on the foxes, of course, but they gave us enough grace. Would have done, if it hadn't been for that bitch last night . . .' Phyllida shivered at the venom in the voice, the first sign of emotion, and this time Kendrick's smile was reassuring and Peter pressed her hand.

'Frank had to think himself, then, into the frame of mind Hargreaves was in, and go with him to the police and then hire the private eye. Frank talked a lot to the dick and the police about the men from the art class, and when he learned they'd gone to the Fountains Hotel the night before the women died he thought it was the best joke he'd ever heard. So everything was going great.'

'So why were you going to kill Sally Hargreaves?' Kendrick asked.

'Frank had thought she didn't know about the relationship between his wife and her mother, but when she made the scene after the funeral he realised she did. He took me into the men's room at the wake and told me Sally was losing control and we'd have to act fast. *I'd* have to act, he had to have his overnight alibi and he'd get a pro in. Frank was losing control himself, he was half crazy, I had to do what he said or he'd have given us both away.'

There was a moment of silence, then DS Wetherhead's voice. 'You're wondering what to say about the gasman's kit, aren't you, sir?'

'All right, I've used it in the past. Successfully, you'll find nothing against me on your computer. I went round to the flat so as to get my bearings. I'd have let myself in if the old lady hadn't answered the bell What happened to her? Frank told me to take her out as well last night, but he didn't tell me about the bitch with the gun.'

'Because he didn't know about her,' Kendrick said. 'How did you get the key to the flat?'

'Frank knew Carol's daughter had given a key to her mother, and the tail Frank put on the women led him there a few times in the afternoons.' Phyllida shuddered, glad that Sally wasn't with them and determined she would never know. 'So the key on her ring he didn't recognise had to be the key to the flat. We left everything intact in both bags when we'd been through them to make it look as if a blackmailer had been searching for the note, but I took that key on Frank's instructions, he thought it might come in handy, and it did. And that bitch did for everything. If I could get my hands—'

Kendrick was sitting near the machine and switched it off. 'There's nothing more, really.'

'Thank you for letting us hear it,' Mrs Sunbury drawled.

'Thank *you* for all you did.'

'I almost got Sally Hargreaves killed. I was responsible for her outburst, because I let her see in church how personally sorry for her a stranger was.' She couldn't move on unless she told him. Mrs Sunbury's voice was a help.

Kendrick didn't hesitate. 'You could hardly have anticipated Miss Hargreaves' reaction, Miss Bowden. And you made restitution.'

'Why?' Peter demanded of Phyllida next morning, when Steve and Jenny had run out of plaudits and left them on their own. 'Why do you think Frank Trenchard went so far? Setup murder, and then again just to keep a secret?'

'Because his enormous male ego had been assaulted. I felt that ego, Peter. Even when he was just sitting with his head on his chest his blokishness seemed to me to fill the room. I can imagine the rage of a man like that when he discovers not only that his wife has been unfaithful, but that he's been cuckolded by a woman. That's why he killed Carol. And he wanted to kill Sally because the prospect of it coming out, of the world laughing at him and pitying him, wasn't to be borne. When he realized she knew, and how temporarily unstable she was, he had to silence her quickly, before she told anyone else. Frank Trenchard's certainty that Matthew Hargreaves didn't know has to be what saved Hargreaves' life.'

'Wickedness like that . . .' Peter went to the window, pushed up the sash, and took a deep breath, and Phyllida looked past him to a sparkling spring morning with a breeze that was creaming the wavelets on a navy blue sea. 'It's hard to understand why.'

'Perhaps because of the genes he shares with Daniel. Maybe we should be thankful Ross is as he is.'

'Kendrick told me the poor sister is as innocent as Hargreaves,' Peter said as he sat down. 'He also told me that Daniel Trenchard lacked the application of his brother. He never really settled to a job until Frank took him on and gave him some responsibility and a regular salary. Which no doubt added a man's gratitude to a boy's hero-worship. You look dreadfully tired, by the way,' Peter went on undiplomatically.

'You sent me home yesterday after we'd seen Kendrick.'

'It obviously wasn't enough. And you had Sally Hargreaves to cope with. I think you should take the rest of today off. And tomorrow.'

'I'm all right, but I'll take today. Thanks.'

'I've hardly had a chance to ask you—how is Sally?'

'Not very good, but at least she's with her father, I took her home when I got back from the police. They'd been put in each other's picture, and Heft them in each other's arms. But I don't know if she'll ever get better.'

'Oh, she will.' Peter looked uncomfortable at the prospect of Sally being unhappy ever after, which Phyllida had learned was in keeping with his invariable reluctance to accept, despite his profession, the open-ended sadness of the world.

She had a second coffee in Reception with Steve and Jenny then went out to her car, parked for once behind the Golden Lion, and drove to Seaminster's botanic garden, thinking on the way about what she had learned the day before at the Hargreaves house, sitting disregarded while the father and daughter talked. Matthew as well as Sally and Frank had known about Carol and Maggie, and like them had been convinced he was the only one who did. Like Frank, too, Matthew had been alerted to the liaison because he knew his wife well enough to know that her reactions to him had changed. But he had carried out his own investigation, and discovered that he loved Carol enough to live with his findings . . .

Phyllida parked where she had parked what seemed a very long time ago, on her one other visit when she was working in the theatre, paid her small due, bought a guidebook, and pushed through the turnstile.

She wasn't sure why she had come, or what she expected, but she found herself happy simply to stroll about in the sunshine, the wind stirring the leaves and her unfettered hair, enjoying the changes of ambience between woodland and wilderness and formal planting, and punctuating her wandering with short stops on invitingly placed seats, where she turned her face to the sun and closed her eyes.

At two o'clock she went into the small restaurant, where there were only a few people still at the tables: She had sometimes seen staff eating late in the restaurants attached to their work place, and the Keeper of the Gardens was alone at one of the tables, just starting on a large grill. Phyllida bought a sandwich and a cup of coffee at the counter, then sat down to face him across two empty tables. He looked as she remembered him, relaxed and serene, and was grateful to herself for having let Fiona Steele tell him she was married. When he looked up from the newspaper beside his plate their eyes met and both of them smiled. Phyllida thought there was approval in his; at least, there was not the indifference she had seen in the eyes of other men who had sought her out when she was in character.

She finished eating before he did, and paused by his table on her way out. 'Forgive me,' she said, nodding towards the photograph on the wall which was enabling her to speak to him, 'but I can't walk past without telling you how much I enjoy your garden. It's a lovely place.'

'Thank you!' He had got to his feet and his face had lit up; she had pleased him. Simply as a member of the public at first, but she thought that as he looked at her he saw her as a person. As Phyllida Moon, it had to be. 'Thank you for telling me, I appreciate it.' Yes, she could see in his eyes that he was aware of her as more than a satisfied customer, and she felt suddenly out of breath. 'Do you visit us regularly?'

'Yes,' she lied. 'Although I sometimes have to be away.'

'So I hope to see you again, Mrs . . .?'

'Miss Moon. Thank you. I hope so too, Dr Pusey.'

Phyllida smiled and moved away. Away from the garden too, it had been enough of a beginning.

When she had parked in her driveway she went back on foot to the promenade, where she leaned on the rail and watched the movement of a blue-green sea, thinking of her imminent TV debut and the end of her anonymity.

So far as other people were concerned. Becoming known as the hero's sister in a TV series wouldn't help her herself to discover who she was, and might actually increase the danger of her disappearing.

When she got back to her house she went slowly through her usual ritual of creating a character: clothes, hair, face, and an inward self to match them.

It was harder than usual, but when she stood, ready, in front of her cheval glass, she found herself looking at an unobtrusively elegant woman who she hoped was Phyllida Moon.

Then she got back into her car and drove inland to the Hargreaves', where Phyllida Moon was expected for supper.

9 781447 256944